BRINGING HOME THE BACON

FARM 2 FORKING
BOOK 4

ERIN MALLON

ABOUT THE BOOK

Everyone in my small town thinks I'm the sweet one in the Bedd family, but after a year of financial drama on our farm and a lifetime of being in my hot brothers' shadows, this kindergarten teacher needs to blow off some steam.

When I meet a sizzling hot reality show chef named Bacon, that steam quickly becomes an inferno, and before I know it, my one-night stand has me screaming, "Yes, Chef!" all night long.

All I wanted was one day to escape my small-town existence, forget my troubles, and live it up in the city.

Well, I got my wish.

You know what else I got?

Pregnant.

Now, I have to face the unforgettable man I left behind.

He's salty that I lied to him and left him while the sheets were still warm. I don't blame him one bit, but the clock is ticking until my little pork belly finishes curing, and I am determined to thaw his heart before that happens.

CHAPTER 1
COLLEEN

"Colleen Bedd, is that you?" a familiar voice calls out the moment I enter The Quick Lick, the only convenience store in our small farming town.

Ugh. Running into my former best friend every time I need basic necessities is anything but convenient. Especially this morning, when all I want to do is get in, get out and get on the road.

"Ginny, you saw me here on Tuesday afternoon," I say as I inch my way toward the snack aisle. "And the Friday before that. Why do you always greet me like I'm a weary world traveler home at last?"

I may be weary, but not because I've been traveling. I can't remember the last time I left the *county*, let alone the country. Ever since my grandad died and we learned how screwed our farm is on the financial front, I've been glued to my grandmother's side. I may as well be one of the soybean stalks planted in the ground at Bedd Family Farm.

But at least *they* get harvested annually.

Me? My roots are permanent.

Thank god I get a temporary change of scenery today. I can't get my butt on that bus fast enough. I just need to survive another Ginny encounter first.

Ginny abandons her perch at the cashier stand to follow me past the pretzels and potato chips. "I miss you, girl! That's all I'm trying to say. Come on, gimme the scoop. You used to tell me everything!"

I grab a bag of trail mix and toss it in my basket, some last-minute fuel for the three-hour ride to NYC. "Well, I'm heading into the city today for—"

"The Fork Lick Elementary teacher trip. Right, right." She sounds bored and doesn't even take a pause before panting, "How's Samuel?"

There it is.

She wasn't actually asking what's new with *me*. She wants to know about my brother.

Scratch what I said a moment ago about Ginny being my former best friend. That was too generous. She's demoted. Ginny Quick shall now forever be known as "The Girl Who Dated My Hot Twin For a Hot Split Second in High School, and Has Spent the Better Part of the Last Eight Years Relentlessly Probing Me for Information on Him."

I realize that title needs some work, but the sentiment is sound.

Damn, this shit is irritating. And insulting too. I'd like to think that having four hot brothers is the least interesting thing about me, yet that seems to be the only aspect of my life anyone ever wants to talk about.

Particularly the ladies.

If it's not Ginny pining over her unrequited love for Sam, it's the women at Tiddy's Bar cackling over how Alex can "make them *Udderly Creamy* any day"—that's the name of his farm—while I struggle not to lose my lunch.

Oh, and my broody brother Ethan? He screws up my social life too. One time in ninth grade, I invited a bunch of girls over to Gran's house to work on a Shakespeare project, and we got absolutely nothing done. Why, you ask? Because they took one look at my sweaty oldest brother entering the kitchen after working the land with Grandad and spent the afternoon launching a fan club instead: *Elizabethans for Ethans*. That was a dark day in young Colleen's life.

"Shh, shh, shh." Ginny points at the speakers in the corner of the store where the first strains of an electric guitar are playing.

"I didn't say anything," I grumble and grab a bottle of water from the cold case.

"Jackson's latest and greatest is playing!" She headbangs to the music.

As if I hadn't already suffered enough being the only female Bedd sibling, Jackson— my sweet, nerdy little brother who I was counting on to *stay* sweet and nerdy—decided to evolve into a hot musician. His career shot into the stratosphere a few years ago, so now I am the lucky sister of three hot farmers and a world-famous rock star too.

"Oh girl, you must be sooooo proud," Ginny croons.

I am proud. Of all of them.

But just once, I'd like someone to see me for *me*.

"Do you think Jackson will go to the Grammys this year?"

"I don't know, Ginny."

"Do you think Ethan and Alex have officially buried the hatchet?"

"I don't know, Ginny."

"Most importantly, do you think Samuel and this Diane woman will last? Because between you and me, I don't think she's the right fit for him and—"

"I DON'T FUCKING KNOW, GINNY!"

Her mouth falls open.

I don't blame her for being shocked. Most people in this town would be surprised to hear Fork Lick's "kind and cutesy kindergarten teacher" dropping an F-bomb in the snack aisle of the local market. But sometimes a girl gets pushed too far.

"Yikes," Ginny says. "Testy today, huh? Is it your time of the month or something?"

Did she just say that to me?

"Ginny. There is little hope for us as a society if even *women* are saying things like that to women. I apologize for snapping at you, but—"

She bops herself on the forehead like she's such a silly goose. "No, that's right! You bought tampons here two weeks ago, so you must be entering your ovulation phase now. My bad."

I'm gonna lose it.

Life in a small town is slowing but steadily killing me. Everyone knows every bit of everyone else's business. *I* didn't even know I was ovulating, but freaking Ginny Quick does? Seriously, it's too much.

I'm saved by the bell when the front door chimes and Ginny scurries to the front of the store to greet her next victim, er, customer.

In hopes of getting my anger under control before dealing with Ginny again, I take a meandering route to the checkout and find myself stopped in the Family Planning aisle. Yes, that's actually how this section is labeled. I'd talk to the owner about changing the antiquated phrasing, but that would involve intentionally engaging Ginny, and it's just not worth it.

Pads, tampons, condoms, lube, pregnancy tests, diapers... it's all here. Gosh, there are so many varieties of condoms these days. When was the last time I even needed one of these suckers? Has it been a full year? I think back to last summer and my tryst with Bob, the guy I met in Climax—the closest big town about a half hour from here. On second thought, can you call something a tryst if it was actually only six weeks of vanilla sex and bland conversation? Probably not. We may have met in Climax, but our sex life was devoid of any such thing.

"Whatcha got there, Miss Bedd?" a little voice chirps beside me, and I instinctively toss the condom box back on the rack like it's on fire.

One of my former students stands there, eyes twinkling and gap-toothed smile beaming.

"Kayleigh! Sweetie! Hi!" I squeak. "I was, um, I was just looking for some, um… some, uh… some paper and some primary-colored washable markers for my classroom!"

There. Those are respectable items for a kindergarten teacher to be browsing.

"Well, you're in the wrong aisle, then, Miss Bedd," the six-year-old says, full of sass. "Markers and crayons are in the School Supplies section, silly." She leans closer and sounds out the words on the box I was just holding a moment ago, just like I taught her. "What's… 'Ribbit For Her Pleasure'? Is that some kind of frog game?"

I then notice Kayleigh's mother farther down the aisle, juggling her eight-month-old son in a baby carrier and grabbing a pack of diapers from the shelf. Her face pales in horror when her daughter's question registers.

"Yup, it's a frog game!" I practically ribbit myself, I'm so embarrassed.

Get me out of here.

The little girl gasps. "I love frogs! Frogs are my favorite animal! Mommy! Can we get 'Ribbit for Her Pleasure' and play it at home?"

I lock eyes with her mother, who seems to be on pause, her mouth open and the diaper pack in her hand frozen midair on its way to her basket.

"No!" I shout.

Kayleigh startles.

"It's, uh. It's just a… a grown-up game, sweetie," I sputter. "Can you remind me where the school supplies are, Kayleigh?" I point two aisles over. "They're that way, right?"

"Right!" Kayleigh nods proudly. Little kids love the rare

opportunity to teach grown-ups something, so I'm going to use this to my advantage.

"Cool if she accompanies me?" I ask her poor mother who is finally getting breath back into her lungs. "I'll bring her right back."

She nods. When Kayleigh skips in front of me, I turn back to her mom one more time and mouth, "I'm sooooo sorry," then hustle to catch up with her kid.

"Voilà!" Kayleigh says when we reach the school supplies. "My dad always says that word. Isn't it fun? Say it. Voilà!"

"Voilà! Yeah, that is fun. Okay great. Now I know where everything is. Thanks a million, sweetheart. Let's bring you back to your mom."

"But aren't you gonna get some?" she asks.

"Some... what?"

Her little eyebrows smoosh together in confusion. "You said you were looking for paper and primary color washable markers."

"Right," I sigh. "I did."

For the record, this isn't the first or even the hundredth time I've been in a situation like this. When you've taught kindergarten for six years straight in the same small town, like I have, you know *all* the children. More to the frightening point, *they* know *you*. Which sounds lovely in theory, right? Well, consider this: it is impossible to live your life. You can't get the slightest bit tipsy at the local bar without a parent seeing you and giving you a disapproving look. Virtually anyone you find attractive and consider pursuing romantically is inevitably related to one of your students, past or present. And, as today's lesson has taught us, it's almost guaranteed that if you need to purchase a product for any of the primal functions of your body—be it menstrual, sexual, or intestinal—an adorable child will catch you in the act and embarrass the hell out of you.

Early elementary teachers are put on this absurd pedestal of purity.

And as much as I love my job, I want to get off.

The pedestal, I mean! I want to "get off" the *pedestal*. I didn't mean I want to "get off" in the other sense of the—whatever. This is clearly not the time or the place for such thoughts.

One look at Kayleigh's proud face and I know the only way to put this encounter behind me is to actually make the purchase she expects me to make. With classes starting next week, the back-to-school shopping rush is behind us, and The Quick Lick's shelf looks pretty bare. So I pick up the only heavy-ass jumbo pack of printer paper they have left and a four-pack of markers. Not exactly what I want to lug with me on a daytrip to New York City.

But a girl's gotta do what a girl's gotta do.

With only ten minutes left until the bus departs, I return my adorable former student to her mom and run my purchases to the checkout. I'm not sure why, but I apologize to Ginny again as she scans my things.

"I didn't mean to be so harsh before, Gin. I'm sorry."

"It's okay, Collie. If I were about to lose my farm, I'd probably be acting like a biatch too."

I take my things from her a bit rougher than necessary and place them directly in my backpack. "Please don't call me Collie. Or biatch," I say as I pay her. "And we're not losing the farm."

"That's not what *The Scuttlebutt* says." Ginny purses her lips and hands me my change.

"Yeah, well, I wouldn't listen to scuttlebutt if I were you," I say, my smile as sweet as pie.

"No, *The* Scuttlebut." She shoves a flier at me just as I'm turning to leave. "Read it! I'd like to hear what you think! We're quickly becoming our town's most reliable news source!" she shouts as I hustle toward the exit.

When I step into the blistering August sun, the fluorescent flier in my hand blares up at me so brightly I need to shield my eyes. "The Scuttlebutt" is emblazoned across the top in an old-timey font with the subtitle "Ginny Quick Gives You All the Dirt on Fork Lick."

Dear god.

The town gossip has created her own official gossip magazine. And the entire front page is dedicated to "The Bedd Family Financial Drama."

I can't board that chartered bus fast enough.

Seriously.

Get me out of this freaking town.

CHAPTER 2
BACON

"PLACES IN FIVE," OUR STAGE MANAGER APRIL SAYS AS SHE breezes past me.

"Thank you, five," I mumble. It's an old habit from the one and only play I performed in as a teen. The intense stage fright I endured every night of that production ensured I never stepped foot on a stage again.

Until now.

My hands are shaking just as hard as they did back then, and I'm sweating like a pig, which I suppose is appropriate, considering my nickname is Bacon.

That's right, *Bacon*. I'm a grown man, and everyone in my life calls me Bacon. The nickname started in high school. I hated it at first, but here I am, over fifteen years later, proudly introducing myself like I'm a celebrity pork product—no last name necessary. Somewhere along the line, I got used to it.

Unlike my short stint as a high school thespian, I'm not playing George in *Of Mice and Men* today. Luckily, I'm just me. But I'm a contestant on a reality cooking show called *Yes, Chef.* Which is so foreign to me, it may as well be Shakespeare. Set on the moon.

The cooking part is easy. And up until now, we've filmed each episode on a closed set, so my nerves have been relatively calm. But today, we're filming in front of a live audience for the first time.

I've never felt more out of my element in my life.

I auditioned for this show as a joke. A dare, really. Over a few beers one night, my buddy Trent said I needed to "shake things up" in my life and try something new. He's a hard guy to say no to, so I gave it a go and—what do you know—I booked it.

I'm just as surprised as anyone. I am not a reality TV guy. All those shows whipping up drama for drama's sake? No, thank you. I've had enough real-life theatrics to last me a lifetime. My family wrote its own salacious story without the help of producers or network TV.

Now, I'm the only one left in that family.

I'm alone.

"Hey, April?" I call after her as she juggles a million tasks during those last precious minutes before the cameras start rolling. "My buddy Trent Cartwright is supposed to be in the audience today as my guest. Do you know if he made it?"

I squint at the overhead monitor, which shows the studio audience getting settled on the other side of the curtain. I don't see him. Dammit, I wanted him here for this one. Today's show determines who makes it into the top ten. I can't believe I'm saying this, but I really want to be one of those contestants.

"Trent Cartwright? The thriller writer?" April says, eyes widening.

"Yeah," I say proudly. "Have you read anything he's written?"

"Of course! *Only the Lonely? Wake Me When it's Over? The Sticking Point?* He's amazing. His twists are legendary!"

I nod and smile. "I'll tell him you said so."

If he ever gets here.

April quickly scrolls the guest list on her tablet. "Sorry, hon. He hasn't checked in."

Just as I go to power down my phone, a call comes through from the man himself.

"Speak of the devil." Even I can hear the relief in my voice when I answer.

"You were speaking of me, were ya?" Trent chuckles.

"Eh. More like talking shit about you."

"To whom?"

"Anyone who will listen, buddy," I joke. "Hey, you up for some constructive criticism, sir?"

"Always."

"Cool it with the *whom* stuff, will ya? I know it's correct grammar and all, but between you and me, it just makes you sound like a punk. A pretentious punk."

"Noted, Porky." Trent laughs.

"I am Bacon." I do my best Christian Bale Batman impression. "Not Porky."

"Just trying to keep you grounded, man. It was one thing when the girls in high school called you Bacon because you're 'so sizzling hot.'" He does an impression of a teenage girl. "But now that you're making national news, I gotta help you keep your ego in check."

"Says the guy the New York Times just called 'The Next James Patterson.' If we need to worry about anyone's ego, it's yours." I scan the monitor one more time. "Where are you? The show is going to start any minute."

"I know. I'm so sorry but—"

"You can't make it," I say.

"I can't make it." The regret is heavy in Trent's tone. "My new draft got leaked. Some idiot posted all these spoiler videos that are going viral, so my editor called an emergency meeting. That meeting went way longer than expected, and I'm still way the hell downtown." He sighs. "You know I'd be there if I could."

"I know you would."

And I do. Trent's career is kicking into a higher gear, so

he's busier than ever, but I know that he's always in my corner no matter what. This is a guy who literally gave me the clothes off his back and put a roof over my head when I didn't have anything.

"I'll be at the next one," he says. "Promise."

"If there is a next one."

"Are you kidding me? You're a shoo-in for the top ten."

My fellow contestants gather by the curtain in their white coats and hats, looking way more self-assured than I feel.

"How do you figure?" I know I'm fishing for compliments right now, but I don't care. I need a confidence boost if I'm going to get back on that stage in a few minutes.

"For one thing, you're an amazing cook." He clears his throat. "Excuse me. *Chef.*"

"Thank you for finally getting the terminology right," I say with faux seriousness.

"Also, you're killin' these food challenges every single week!"

"I thank you again."

"And finally…"

"Yes?" I stretch out the word.

"Well, don't let it go to your head, but…" He hesitates again, then rushes through the compliment. "You're charismatic as fuck on that screen, my dude. America loves you."

I laugh. "That was painful for you to say, wasn't it?"

"Hurt like a bitch, yeah."

April joins the contestants at the curtain, adjusts the mouthpiece on her headset and speaks with authority. "Alright, everyone. Places!"

"Trent, I gotta go." I lower my voice as I move toward the curtain

"Okay. Bust a nut, buddy."

"Bust a *nut*?" I whisper.

I swear I hear Trent shrug over the phone. "I dunno!

Someone told me saying 'good luck' is actually *bad* luck. And apparently, 'break a leg' isn't much better."

"So you went with 'bust a nut'?"

"Hey, I'm just a writer. I never said I was good with words." He pauses. "How about… go out there and remember who you are. How's that?"

Remember who I am.

"That's, uh, that's pretty good, pal," I say, and dammit, my eyes get misty. "Thanks. Catch ya on the flip side, yo." I end the conversation with him like I always do.

"Catch ya on the flip side," he repeats as expected.

We hang up. I power down my phone and hit my mark on the stage.

I blow out a breath and bounce on my toes, like an athlete getting ready for the big game. Only in this case, I'm a reality show chef about to make a chocolate soufflé.

April gives our light and sound technicians the signal. A second later, the curtain lifts. We walk onstage, and the voice of our show announcer floods the auditorium.

"Ladies and gentleman, welcome to *Yes, Chef!* the cooking show where anything can happen! Allow me to introduce you to our contestants."

———

Thirty minutes later, the whisk flies out of my grip and lodges itself directly into the cleavage of our voluptuous host while chocolate splatters all over her skin. Her sequin dress is speckled too.

"Goodness!" She winks at the camera. "No one told me I was standing in the splash zone!"

This gets a solid laugh from the studio audience.

Our host, Mairin Stapleton, was an actress on a teen show back in the late 90s and now makes the rounds hosting reality shows like this one. She has a lot of practice charming a live audience. Me? I can't get my heart to stop pounding or my hands to stop shaking.

She visits each contestant at least once per episode for some banter while we cook.

I know these chats are a good opportunity for America to get to know me better; I just can't help wishing I could skip this part and cook quietly. Unfortunately, that's not what I signed up for with *Yes, Chef!*

Despite what people say about reality shows being one-hundred percent scripted, that's not the case with this one. I'd give anything to have a script right now because this awkward bit of physical comedy was definitely not planned.

"I'm so sorry," I grab a dish towel from my workstation. Before I can think better of it, I start dabbing at her chest.

She takes that opportunity to wink into the camera and say, "Buy a girl dinner first, will ya, Bacon?"

I pull my hand back like I've been burned, cueing another roar of laughter from the studio audience.

My face turns ten shades of red.

Why am I like this?

I love cooking, but I'm more of a behind-the-scenes kind of guy. It's always been the easiest way for me to take care of people and show them my gratitude.

Cooking for votes feels strange.

"So, Bacon," Mairin says. "As you know, this is a big show. How you perform during today's challenge will determine if you make our Top Ten."

"Well, I guess we can kiss that goodbye then, huh?" I gesture to the chocolate still coating her silver sequins.

The audience laughs.

"Don't be silly. I never object to a handsome guy splattering me with sauce." Mairin gives another wink to the camera.

How she's pulling off all this obvious innuendo on a

network show is a mystery to me, but I guess what they say is true: sex sells.

Mairin continues. "Over the past nine episodes, you've shown a particular affinity for 'comfort foods.' Your chicken potpie in our series premiere had the whole country clucking. And viewers are still writing in asking to sample your Sloppy Joe sliders. Who do you credit for teaching you how to cook?"

"The streets of Philadelphia," I say, then realize how stupid that sounds. "The *actual* streets, not the Bruce Springsteen song. Though damn, that's a great song. Gotta love Bruce, am I right? Shit, can I say damn on network TV?"

Mairin smiles tightly. "Damn is debatable. But shit is definitely not allowed."

"Oh fuck, I'm sorry."

"Whoo-eee!" she says to the studio audience and garners another laugh from them. "Good thing we're not broadcasting live, friends! As they say in showbiz, 'we'll get it in post'!"

I'm a deer in headlights at this point.

Mairin takes pity on me and whispers, "You can head back to your workstation, sweetums."

I nod gratefully and haul ass back to my oven. I place my bowl on the counter and run the chocolate-covered whisk under the faucet. To my left and my right, my fellow contestants are a flurry of activity. They're mixing and sautéing and flambéing at warp speed, but I've shifted into slow motion.

It's no surprise I rambled about Bruce Springsteen a moment ago. He's been on my mind lately. I read this great interview with him once where he said he still gets nervous before every show. He explained that the nerves aren't a negative thing. They're just an indicator that he cares. According to Bruce, we all have a choice when stage fright hits us. We can call it nerves, or we can call it excitement.

I'm still working on it, Bruce.

I really do attribute my cooking skills to the streets of Philadelphia. I started cooking for my mom and me in the third grade, when it became clear she couldn't handle caring for us herself. From the age of sixteen on, I worked forty-hour weeks in restaurants big and small all over the city while simultaneously going to school, managing homework, and making sure my mom had everything she needed at home.

My hands didn't shake back then.

Life was by no means perfect in those early days—not by a long shot—but at least I knew where I belonged. I knew where I was needed. Now, it feels like I'm floating with no sense of where I can land.

I didn't realize how much I counted on having Trent in the audience today. Without him in that crowd, I can only focus on the cameras and the blinding lights. All I can think about are the thousands—maybe millions?—of people who will watch this in a few days and judge me from their couches, voting on whether I deserve to stay or go.

It's official: I am not cut out for this.

During the next commercial break, I'll tell the producers I quit. Big potential prize money or not, it's not worth feeling this anxious every time I step onstage.

As I place my hand on the oven knob and turn it back down to zero, my eye catches something unexpected in the audience.

A gorgeous blonde in a mint green sundress is staring at me, her eyes bright and her smile warm. She's holding a sign. I squint beyond the glaring stage lights to read the text.

You and I Would Be Sizzlin' Together.

I read it twice to make sure I'm not hallucinating her. She could be a mirage. She's that gorgeous, and I'm that desperate for something—or someone—to anchor me. I laugh, point at myself, and mouth, "Who, me?"

She nods, her blond curls bouncing on her bare shoulders. She holds a finger up, silently telling me to wait before rooting through her bag. Luckily, our host has focused on another contestant right now, so the cameras aren't directed at me. I busy myself whisking the concoction for my chocolate soufflé again—no splattering this time—and pour it into small baking tins.

I peek up at her, and she's busy scribbling another note.

When I slide the soufflé into the oven, I realize something.

My hands have stopped shaking.

My breathing has evened out.

My heart is still pounding, but the pounding no longer feels like panic.

It feels like excitement. Just like Bruce said.

I catch movement out of the corner of my eye. That same knockout of a girl is beaming that beautiful smile at me again, and she's holding up a new sign.

Meet Me at the Stage Door, Stud.

I turn my oven knob back up to 360.

Looks like I'm cookin' again.

CHAPTER 3
COLLEEN

MEET ME AT THE STAGE DOOR, STUD?!

I stand on Fifty-seventh Street behind a silver barricade with a dozen or so random audience members. I'm staring at white stenciled letters spelling out "Stage Door" and wondering what the hell came over me in there.

One second, I was unassuming kindergarten teacher Colleen Bedd locking eyes with a man in a chef's hat. A moment later, I was a wild woman, scribbling suggestive signs and propositioning him from the third row.

Though if I'm being honest with myself? It didn't *feel* wild or out of control.

It was the exact opposite feeling.

I knew—I just *knew*—I needed to connect with this man. For once in my life, I didn't think. I just acted. My body bypassed my brain at that moment, and I operated from some primal setting I didn't even know I had.

It felt fantastic.

But now I'm standing here melting on the sidewalk in the late New York City summer sun and doubting all my decisions. One by one, his fellow contestants exit through the big metal door. Still no sign of the man they call Bacon. A few of the chefs sign autographs before hopping into the Town Cars.

Wow. My grandmother loves this show, but I didn't know it was that big of a deal. Seems it's way more popular than I realized.

Ten more minutes pass and now I'm the only one left standing here other than a security guard and the random New Yorkers hurrying past. Clearly, he's not coming. He must have assumed I was a crazed fan—do cooking show contestants have crazed fans?—and slipped out a side exit to avoid me.

Message received, fella.

If I hurry, maybe I can catch up with the rest of the teachers for lunch and shopping. I turn and start heading down Fifty-seventh Street, pulling out my phone to text my coworkers.

"Leaving so soon?" a deep male voice calls out from behind me.

It's him.

I halt in place, but I don't turn around just yet.

"Places to go, people to see. You know how it is," I sass over my shoulder. The energy this man brings out of me is something else.

"Huh. Your sign implied you wanted to see *me*," he says. His voice oozes confidence and calm.

I'm still facing away from him. "I *did*, but you kept me waiting, so I'm not sure I'm interested anymore. Don't you know it's rude to keep a girl waiting?"

"Hmm. Maybe you'll let me make it up to you, then." His voice is much closer now.

He's right behind me.

I finally turn, and my breath catches at the sight of him. The chef's coat and hat are gone. He's now wearing a light blue button-up shirt, sleeves rolled to his elbows, and tan pants that hug him in all the right places.

He chuckles. "Did you just check me out?"

"So what if I did?" I say and boldly take a step closer to

him. "Surely, you checked me out too."

"Of course I did, but I made sure I did that before you turned around."

"Well, that's not fair," I complain. "I wasn't afforded that same opportunity to peruse the merchandise."

Merchandise? Did I just call this man merchandise?

He must not know what to make of me because he just stands there, eyes narrowed and looking so damn sexy.

"What's good for the goose is good for the gander, right?" I say and instantly regret it. My gran always says that phrase. I'm not sure it even makes sense in this context, and it's certainly not sexy.

He surprises me when he says, "By all means, lady… peruse." He pivots away from me and strikes a pose accentuating his rear end.

He's so funny. Part of me wants to crack up, though the larger part of me is fully committed to this role-play we seem to be doing. This is amazing. I said I wanted to be someone else for one day, and that's exactly what's happening. I have no idea who I am right now, and it's exhilarating!

"I'm perusing the hell outta you, stud." His broad back, trim waist, and taut butt are all sorts of sexy.

"Like what you see?" he says, still facing away from me.

I realize this is the first time I've ever set my sights on a guy and actively pursued him. Up until now, I've been so passive in my dating life. Well, not today. Today, I'm a woman who goes after what she wants.

I close the distance between us and wrap my arms confidently around his waist, you know, like I do this sort of thing every day.

"Mmm," I hum. "Very much."

I press my breasts to his muscular back. He sucks in a breath. When he places a warm hand on top of mine and caresses my knuckles with a calloused thumb, it sends a shiver over my skin even though it must be nearly ninety degrees out here.

I tighten my hold on him, my hands longing to slip inside his shirt to run down the delicious abs he clearly has hiding under there.

This is wild. I'm engaged in a bizarre mating ritual on the sidewalks of New York City, and no one is giving me a second glance!

I love this city.

I inhale the scent of gel in his dark hair and the fresh soap on his tan skin. "You showered, huh? That's why you kept me waiting?"

He loosens my hold and turns around to face me. Seeing those chocolate-brown eyes this close is startling. "Well, I couldn't take a beautiful girl out on a date smelling like cooking spray and sweat, could I?"

"I mean, you *could,*" I say. "Don't get me wrong, I appreciate the attention to detail, but..." I lower my voice and crook my finger for him to come even closer. When he's close enough to kiss, I whisper in his ear, "I'm a sure thing, stud."

Stud. What a word. I've never in my life called someone a stud until today. And suddenly, it's my word of choice when it comes to him?

Where did that even come from?

I flashback to nearly two decades ago. It was a few years before my parents' accident. I must have been around eight. My mom and I were watching an old DVD of *Grease.* She loved that movie. I'm guessing because her name was Sandy too. When you're one of five kids and your parents are super in love—a.k.a. borderline obsessed with each other—like mine were, it's hard to get quality one-on-one time with your mom, so I was in heaven that day. I remember being confused by that pivotal scene at the end of the movie, though. It made no sense to me why Danny was so mean to Sandy when she was sweet and wore her pretty yellow skirt and sweater set earlier, and then he worshipped at her feet when she was kind of rude, wearing a tight black leather outfit and puffing a cigarette. But then she said, "Tell me about it, stud," and something must have clicked in my little kid brain and stored information away for the future. That "stud" unlocked all of Sandy's power! After she called Danny "stud," there were suddenly no lines for the carnival rides, the boy she loved was literally chasing her, and her entire small town broke out in song to celebrate her. Her car even learned how to fly!

Stud is a magical word.

A guy with a briefcase yells at us for blocking the sidewalk, so I back up against the building to clear the path. The object of my affection follows me just like Danny Zuko did and—oh my god—he does that thing where he cages me in by bracing his arm on the wall! I've always wanted a guy to pull out this move, but they never do!

"Is your name really Bacon?" I ask in as sultry a tone as I can muster.

"It is, and it isn't," He bows his head down so his pillowy lips can skim my neck. I lift my chin to give him easier access and revel in his trim beard's gentle scratch against my cheek.

"What does that mean, stud?" I breathe.

He chuckles. "It means that, yes, everyone calls me Bacon, but you won't find that name on my birth certificate."

"What name would I find on your birth certificate, stud?"

Okay, I think I'm overdoing it with the stud thing now.

He pulls back from me a few inches and cocks his head playfully. "You're calling me stud an awful lot."

My cheeks heat. "Sorry, stud. I mean— I know I am. I'll stop. Sorry."

"Nothing to be sorry about. It's cute. I, uh, I don't tell anyone my real name until I get to know them better. But I'd like to get to know you better." He takes that opportunity to brush a loose strand of my hair behind my ear. "Can you work with that?"

I can work with the way his touch keeps sending tingles down my body.

I'm at a loss for words, so I just nod.

"What is your name?" he asks.

What *is* my name? It doesn't have to be Colleen today, right? Today, I can be anyone I want. Besides, if he's going to call himself Bacon, I'll call myself...

"Cookie," I say. "My name is Cookie."

"Really?" His normally low voice pitches upward.

"You sound surprised."

"I guess you don't seem like a Cookie."

"Why?" I run a finger all the way down his chest and grab his belt buckle in my fist when I reach his waist. "You don't want to take a bite of my ooey-gooey center?" I give his belt a tug to draw him close to me again.

I know the voice coming out of me is mine, but I barely recognize it. It comes from somewhere deep inside me. A place that's bold and brave and—if I'm being honest— bizarre. No one ever told me that letting your freak flag fly is the key to feeling free. Now that I know? I'm going to wave my weirdness at him like it's my damn job.

"No, I *do* want to bite you," he says. "If you, uh, if you consent to being bitten."

"I consent, Bay-CAHN. I consent soooo hard," I practically purr. I stand on my tiptoes and nip his earlobe. "Oh, and for the record, *I* bite too."

He wraps his arms around my lower back and holds me tight against him. His hardness presses into me, and I have never wanted to be alone with someone more in my life.

"God, you smell good." He buries his face in my hair. Then he pulls back slightly to make eye contact. "Did you just pronounce my name Bay-CAHN?"

"I sure did." I punctuate my words with a double squeeze of his ass.

"May I ask why?" He chuckles.

I give him a slight shrug. "It sounds sexier somehow."

"Works for me, Cookie."

Another warm tingle rushes down my spine at hearing him call me Cookie again. It's so silly, but I freaking love it, and I've decided I never want to be called Colleen again.

"What do you say? You wanna get out of here?" He flashes me that killer smile and offers his arm.

I take it.

"You bet I do, Bay-CAHN. Let's get the hell out of here."

CHAPTER 4
BACON

NEXT THING I KNOW, I'M IN THE BACK OF A BLACK SUV, DRY humping with a cookie. I mean a woman. A woman named Cookie.

The show provides each contestant with a private car after filming. It's a nice perk. A lot of nice perks come from being on this show: catered meals from the best restaurants in New York City, unlimited show merch, free tickets to Broadway plays…and apparently, the opportunity to make out with gorgeous women in the back seats of cars.

When we entered the car a few moments ago, I said to the chauffeur, "Just drive." You know, like how they do in the movies? The guy just rolled his eyes and put up the privacy partition. I guess he's used to people getting it on in his back seat.

I, however, am not used to this. Not at all.

I've always gone the "perfect gentleman" route when it comes to women. I pay for dinner. I open doors. I try to ask thoughtful questions and really get to know someone before things get physical. Trouble is, up until now, all that gentlemanly activity has gotten me nowhere.

Last summer, I decided to stop dating entirely. I figured I'd rather be at home alone with a great book and a cold beer than out with a woman when there's no spark. Before I knew it, I hadn't had sex in a full year, something that horrified Trent.

But the connection between Cookie and me was instant. And I don't mean just physically. The first moment I saw her holding that sign, she somehow managed to light me up and calm me down simultaneously. I recognize how crazy this sounds, but something in me shouted that this girl is special.

"I don't usually do things like this," I say between kisses.

"Neither do I," she pants and digs her nails into my back. She stops abruptly and says, "Scratch that. Actually, yes, I do. I do things like this all the time."

I hesitate. "All the time?"

She nods. "Mm-hmm. Yeah, I get around, buddy! Is that a problem?"

"Uh… No? I guess not?"

Who am I to judge, right?

She leans against the door and stretches her legs out along the seat. "Is this a mega SUV or something? It's so spacious back here." She sounds impressed.

"It is, isn't it?" I prowl toward her across the seat like a predatory cat, but she holds up a finger to stop me before I make contact.

"Think you can stand in here?" She peers curiously at the car's ceiling, which is certainly higher than one would expect.

"No, I'm too tall to stand, but I can rise on my knees like this. Why?"

The second I kneel on the plush back seat, she whips off my belt, unzips my pants, and shucks them down to my knees, revealing my bulging gray boxer briefs.

"Oooh. Me likey," she says with a smile.

"Thank you? You, uh, wow. You shucked the hell out of my pants."

"You should see what I can do with corn," she says as she approaches my crotch, then freezes.

"Corn?" I say.

"Yeah, well, that's what I do, Bay-CAHN." She dips a hand into my boxer briefs, grabs ahold of me, and starts stroking up and down. "I'm a shucker. I'm a shucker and a fucker."

What she's doing feels fantastic, but I can't help it. The shucker/fucker line makes me laugh my ass off. Clearly, that wasn't the response she was looking for because she pulls her hand back and resumes sitting by the door opposite me, the light in her eyes from a minute ago dimmed.

I'm literally on my knees with my pants down, feeling like an ass.

"I'm sorry, Cookie. I didn't mean to... You're just so funny," I say, catching my breath and pulling up my pants. "And adorable. I really like you, Cookie."

Her eyes twinkle again. "I like you too."

I slide closer and sit beside her.

"That's a good start," I whisper and place a soft kiss on her neck. "Okay. So far, I know you're drop-dead gorgeous, you kiss like a goddess, and you smell like a dream..."

"What else is there to know?" she jokes.

"Plenty, I'm sure. You live here in the city? Or are you visiting?"

"Yup!" she says and reaches for my dick again.

"Wait, wait, wait," I say softly and move her hand away. "Yup, you live in the city? Or yup, you're visiting?"

I must be an idiot. A beautiful woman wants to pleasure me in the back of an SUV, no questions asked, and I can't just go with the flow. I want—no, I *need*—to know more about her.

"City," she gives me a one-word answer.

"Ah," I say. "I wasn't sure when you mentioned your corn-shucking prowess. Thought maybe you were a country girl."

"NYC farmers' markets are my bitch." She winks.

I laugh. "Can't blame you. I love the one down in Union

Square. I'm also a fan of the one on Columbus between Seventy-seventh and Seventy-ninth. You ever been to those?"

She scoffs. "Of course."

"Okay…" I leave space for her to steer the conversation. She doesn't.

"So, what do you do?" I press. "You know, besides the shucking and the fucking."

"I'm in publishing." She looks out the window when she says it.

"Oh yeah? That's cool. My buddy Trent is an author. What side of things are you on?"

"What side of things?" she asks.

Damn, she's really not forthcoming with information about herself.

"Well, yeah. There are lots of sides to publishing, right? Are you a writer? An agent? A publisher?"

Instead of answering my question, she nibbles my earlobe again and whispers, "What do you say we skip all this get-to-know-you talk and just do what we came here to do?"

You know what? Fuck it.

I'm allowed to have a little fun.

"Alright," I say. "But let's put this driver out of his misery and actually find a private place to land. Where should we go, your place or mine?"

"Yours!" she says with a little too much emphasis.

The seed of doubt bouncing around in my body firmly plants itself in my stomach. It's something I can't ignore. Not after what I went through with my family.

"That's fine. We can definitely go to my place, but, um, is something wrong with your place?"

"No," she says. "Nothing wrong per se. The, uh… my penthouse is being renovated right now, so I'm not really hosting guests at the moment."

"Cookie, you're not already involved with someone, are you?" I ask firmly, no hint of humor this time.

"No, of course not. I would never do that!" Her face is soft, and her eyes are wide.

Call me crazy, but I believe her.

"Okay." I sigh in relief. "Because I need to make something very clear before we go any further: I don't cheat. I don't help others cheat. And there's nothing I hate more in this world than liars." I cup her cheek with my hand, stare deep into her bright blue eyes, and plead with her, "Please don't lie to me."

A silent moment passes that feels like an eternity.

Then she swallows, places a small hand on my cheek, and says, "There's no one else. And I promise, I won't lie to you."

My face slowly splits in a grin. "Excellent." I knock on the privacy partition and say, "Driver? Seventy-fifth and West End, please."

CHAPTER 5
COLLEEN

THE SECOND THE DOOR SLAMS BEHIND US IN BACON'S apartment, we're "off to the races" as Gran would say. Ugh. I really need to stop thinking about my grandmother so much. Especially when I'm in the throes of passion with the hottest man I've ever encountered in real life.

We're currently a tangle of limbs and hands and tongues. And we can't get each other's clothes off fast enough.

"I've never seen—or felt—a bra like this," he pants between kisses. "Is it… wool?"

"Merino wool, yes," I huff as I once again shuck his pants to the floor. This time, we have plenty of room and plenty of privacy, so he kicks the pants aside, and I slide my skirt down my legs as well.

"Did someone handknit this for you?" he asks.

I hesitate for a split second, but I promised the man I wouldn't lie to him, and I meant it. I can't help the lies I've already told. But from here on in, I will be as truthful as humanly possible with him.

"Yeah. My grandma."

Both of us are down to our underwear now. Him in his tight gray boxer briefs that leave very little to the imagination —thank god. And me in a Strawberry Shortcake-themed thong paired with one of the many woolen bras my grand-mother has knit for me over the years. She calls them "Baabara's Boulder Holders."

For the record, Baabara Streisand Bedd is my gran's beloved sheep. Some might argue she's the sixth and most rambunctious Bedd child. But her fibers are plentiful and hearty. I've tried all the underwire and padded cups in the world, and none of them cradle my double Ds as well as that sheep's wool does.

Still, I really wish I'd chosen my undergarments more wisely this morning. In my defense, I thought I was only going to see a cooking show with a group of elementary teachers today. I had no idea this would also be the day I'd embark on my personal sex revolution. Had I known that, I may have worn something more attractive.

I wrap my leg around his muscular thigh. He squeezes my nearly bare ass with both hands, but he's still focused on the damn bra.

"It's so... unique." He gathers my still-covered breasts in his large hands. "And an odd choice for the summer. Don't most women wear bras that are silky? Or cottony?" He pauses. "Is cottony a word?"

"Cottony is a word, yes. It sounds wrong, but it's actually right. While we're on the subject of bras, why don't you take mine off, stud?"

He stays on the subject at hand, continuing to explore my bra with his thumbs. My nipples harden under his touch. Not that he can feel them through this thick-ass wool. "Isn't it itchy?" he asks.

"Sort of. But I don't mind." I'm getting impatient now and lift my breasts higher to encourage him. "Go on hot stuff, take it off."

He lowers to his knees and rubs his stubbly cheek against my cleavage. It's an odd move for sure, but damn, it feels good.

"Gosh, I'm just amazed it gives you the support you need."

Alright, I've had enough.

I run my hands through his dark hair, gather a clump, and give it a playful tug, forcing him to look up at me. "Are we going to keep talking about my bra, Bacon? Or do you plan on taking it off at some point?"

"You don't have to ask me twice," he says with enthusiasm.

"Apparently, I do, sir, since that was the third time I asked."

"Ooh. Sir," he says as he reaches for the ribbon tied behind me. "I like that."

With one pull of that taut pink bow, my breasts tumble free.

Bacon circles the woolen bra over his head like he's preparing a lasso, then lets it sail across the room, his eyes never leaving my chest.

"Wow." His breathing is shallow as I stand there in all my topless glory.

"Wow good?"

"Wow *un-fucking-believable*." He lowers to his knees again —what is it with this guy and getting on his knees for me?— and proceeds to lavish my breasts with attention. His tongue circles the nipple of one breast while his thumb caresses the other.

"Fork me, you're good at that," I moan.

"Fork you?" he says as he moves his talented mouth to my other breast.

"Fork me, shuck me, fuck me, I don't care, just get inside me already, will you?"

Bacon releases my breast and rises to his full height. He must be at least six foot one, so he towers over my tiny five foot three. He doesn't say a word, but a devilish smile crosses his face, and he shakes his head.

"What?" I ask. "Why are you shaking your head at me? You don't want to be inside me?"

"Are you kidding me? I've wanted to be inside you since the moment I spotted you in that studio audience."

"So… what's the problem?"

"No problem." He hoists me up in a fireman carry like I weigh nothing and whispers in my ear, "I just need to take a bite out of your ooey-gooey center first, Cookie." With that, he walks me down a short hallway, takes me into his bedroom, and lowers me onto his king-sized bed.

Three things happen in my mind at that moment. First, I inwardly cringe hearing my words quoted back to me—*bite my ooey-gooey center*? Really? Second, I desperately want to tell him my real name. Cookie felt so fun before, but the more time I spend with this guy, the more I hate that I ever lied to him. And third, I thank my lucky stars that I met this man today.

Bacon slides my thong down my legs. "You're incredible," he says on a reverent exhale as he takes me in, lying there completely exposed to him.

"You are too," I whisper.

And I mean it.

He is.

In one swift motion, he pulls me by the hips so my ass lines up right at the edge of the mattress and my legs dangle over the bedframe. Maintaining eye contact with me, he lowers himself to the ground, lifts my left leg, and gently places it over his shoulder.

"Is this okay?"

When I nod in response, he embarks on a steady path of open-mouthed kisses, starting at my knee, climbing up my inner thigh, taking a delicious detour to tease my hip bone, then he finally makes contact with my clit.

It's official, this man is an expert at pleasing a woman. He starts slow and sensual. He somehow knows exactly what I want, and he's so eager to give it to me. I gasp. I moan. My back arches. He's perfection... and I can't handle it for a single second longer.

Come on, Colleen, let yourself enjoy this.

I try.

But I can't.

I reach down and lift his head.

"What's wrong? Are you okay?" His brown eyes shimmer with concern.

Summon that Cookie energy, girl.

"I'm more than okay," I say with that sass I've been practicing today, then twirl a lock of his hair. "I just can't wait another second to have you on top of me."

He grins. "As you wish, milady." He rises to his full height while I scurry up the mattress and rest my head on one of his plush pillows.

"Here's a question," I say. "Why is it that I'm completely naked while you're standing there in your boxer briefs?"

"Hardly seems fair, does it?" He solves our problem by taking off the last bit of his clothes. His cock finally springs free, and I nearly choke.

"That is... Wow, what you've got there is—Whoooo!" I fan myself comically. "I *really* want that."

He laughs. "Coming right up, miss." He struts confidently to his bedside table, pulls out a condom, then squints at the packaging.

"What are you doing?" I ask.

"Checking the expiration date." He shrugs. "It's been a while."

I know I'm a fully grown woman, and this shouldn't delight me——the fact that he's not with a different woman every night of the week—but it does.

"It's been a while for me, too," I admit.

"Really? I thought you said in the car that you 'get around,'" he says as he tears open the condom wrapper.

"I think I was just trying to impress you," I groan in embarrassment and cover my face. "In reality, I am extremely conservative when it comes to sleeping with people, and I get routinely tested for STDs. It was pretty progressive of you not to judge me for my original statement, though."

"Progressive?" he says. "I don't know about that. I mean, I don't know a man alive who enjoys thinking about the woman he's hot for being with another guy. But any man who judges a woman for taking ownership of her pleasure isn't worth her time. Also, I get routinely tested too. Just last week, in fact. I'm all good."

"Sexy! Geezuz! Everything you say and do is so sexy!"

He flashes me that gorgeous smile as he slides the condom down his cock with both hands, his forearms flexing.

"Even that!" I shout. "Sir, with moves like that, they should hire you to perform in safe sex educational videos! One look at that sexy sex move you just did, and people would wear condoms always and forever!"

He crawls over me on the bed, braces himself on one arm and kisses me softly on the lips. "I appreciate that, but I think I'll stick to cooking."

"Yeah, well you're good at that too," I arch into him while he rains kisses down the column of my throat.

"I'm really glad I met you today," he says.

"Me-too-put-it-in," I mumble, already in ecstasy.

"Me too put it in?" He laughs.

"Yes, please," I huff.

"My pleasure," he says.

Just as Bacon places the head of his truly beautiful cock at my opening… "Daniel" by Elton John blares from the other room.

"Is that your phone?" he asks, but the ringtone quickly stops.

"Uh, yeah, it was. Sorry. I should have put it on silent." I run my nails down his back to get us back on track.

He instantly responds to my touch. "No problem. Where were we?"

"Riiiiight here, I think."

I take him in my hand this time and place him right where I want him. He nudges inside me just an inch. My mouth falls open in pleasure, and… "Daniel" by Elton John blares again from the other room, then stops.

I'm going to kill him.

Bacon pulls away again. "You think maybe someone's trying to get in touch with you?"

"Yeah, maybe, but whatever, he can leave a message."

"He?" Bacon's eyebrows furrow.

Yeah, my twin brother who always knows how to spoil my good time.

But I don't say that. Instead, I grab Bacon's hips and pull him close again, saying, "He, she, they, whoever. Let's just ignore it. All I care about right now is you and me."

"You and me. I like the sound of that." He kisses me on the nose. It's so tender and sweet, I could melt.

But it turns out I don't want tender and sweet right now. Right now, I want to…

The ringtone blares a third time, and this time I am pissed.

"Ughhhhhhhh! Excuse me a moment."

Bacon rolls to his side while I bolt buck naked into the next room.

The phone stops ringing just as I pick it up. A litany of text messages from Sam have all been delivered in the past ten minutes. In rapid succession.

SAM-DAN

Colleen are you okay

Colleen please answer me

Twin-sense is taking over and I'm worried about you

Are you in some kind of danger in NYC

Report back or I'm calling the police

I fire off a text of my own.

Seriously, dude? The police? Simmer down.
I'm fine! I'm having fun with a friend.

The dots on the screen show that he's responding right away.

SAM-DAN

A friend

Which friend

I didn't realize you had a friend who lives in the city

It's possible you don't know everything about me, brother.

SAM-DAN

Possible I suppose but not likely

I'm glad you're okay

See you tonight

Yeah. See you tonight.

What people say about being a twin is true: it's a connection like none other. It's powerful. Beautiful. Mystical even. It can also be extremely irritating. Sam and I have experienced the typical twin stuff you hear about. He can look at me and know what I'm feeling, even when I desperately try to hide my emotions. When we were eleven and he broke his left arm on the school playground, I felt an instant ache in *my* left arm even though I was home sick that day and had no idea what was happening. When we were toddlers learning to talk, I instinctively called him Sam-Dan. This dumbfounded our parents because apparently, while we were in utero, they kept going back and forth on whether to name him Samuel or Daniel. Somehow, I just *knew* that and have always called him Sam-Dan.

Oh and, subconsciously, Sam always knows when I'm about to have sex.

I haven't dared to tell another human—not even Sam—about this phenomenon because it's so beyond bizarre. Honestly, up until today, I couldn't quite believe it myself. But my experience this afternoon proves it. Every single time I've had—or attempted to have—sex, my twin brother has texted me saying his twin-sense is telling me I'm in danger.

Yeah, Sam. In danger of having too many orgasms.

"You're not standing in my way today, brother," I mumble as I power down my phone. "Today, I'm getting mine."

Or maybe not.

Because when I strut back into Bacon's bedroom to join him, he's still deliciously sprawled out in the covers, but he's sound asleep.

CHAPTER 6
COLLEEN

"Mmm." I roll over in my half-asleep state and smile in the dark. Why do I feel so…fantastic? I'm naked, wrapped up in the softest blanket. My breathing is smooth and deep. My mind and body haven't felt this relaxed in months. It's like I'm resting on a warm, beautiful cloud. The cool air carries the faint strains of music and the scent of… bacon?

The food, not the man.

That's when it all comes rushing back. I just had *almost* sex with a man named Bacon.

I bolt upright in an unfamiliar bed. "OHMYGOD, WHAT TIME IS IT?!" The room I'm in is way darker now than it was before. I can't immediately locate my clothes, so I wrap a bedsheet around my naked body and hurry toward the kitchen.

What I see in that kitchen stops me in my tracks. The sexy man I dallied with this afternoon stands at his stove, frying eggs and bacon and listening to acoustic rock. He's wearing a red apron and absolutely nothing underneath. His back is turned to me, so I have an incredible view of his bare, rock-hard ass.

He senses my presence and turns around with a spatula in

hand. "Oh, hi!" he shouts over the music, then quickly lowers the volume. "Have a nice nap?"

"What time is it?" I root around in my purse, find my phone, and power it back on.

"It's, uh…" He checks the electric clock on his stove. "It's five after eight."

"Eight o'clock? At night?!" I shout. The chartered bus arranged by Fork Lick Elementary left five minutes ago. I frantically scroll through the online schedule for public buses heading to Greene County from Port Authority.

It's just as I feared. The last bus leaves in fifteen minutes. I'll never make it.

"Yeah…" he says cautiously. "I know it's nighttime, but I'm a breakfast-for-dinner kinda guy. Is that not okay? I'm happy to make you something else."

"The food is fine!" I wince. "I just missed my—" I stop myself midsentence. I already told him I'm a New Yorker and my penthouse is being renovated, so I can't exactly tell him I missed the last bus back to my little farming town and have no place to go tonight. Not without admitting to him I'm a big fat liar.

My brain cycles through possible ways to get home tonight without blowing my cover. Call one of my brothers to come get me? No way. Find a taxi willing to take a two-and-a-half-hour drive to Upstate New York? I may as well kiss my first week of teacher's pay goodbye.

You'll figure this out, Colleen. You always do. Just like you figured out how to get our farm out of debt. Oh, that's right, you haven't.

"You missed your what?" He waits patiently for my answer.

"Nothing. I, um…" God, he looks good. "I just… I missed my opportunity to have sex with you."

Smooth, girl. Smooth.

Bacon laughs. He has an incredible laugh. "The night is

still young, Cookie."

He winks, then turns back to the stove, giving me that delightful view of his bare butt again. One pull of that red string and that apron would come tumbling down. Somehow, I manage to control myself.

"But I, uh—I do owe you an explanation for that." He arranges two plates of eggs and bacon, sets them on the small marble island in the center of the space, and pulls up two red stools.

"I've been wondering about that. Typically, don't men fall asleep *after* they orgasm?" I joke as I take a seat beside him and pick up a fork. "When I walked in the room, you were sound asleep, pork sword still at half-mast."

He chokes on his eggs. "Excuse me, did you just say I have a pork sword?"

"One hell of a pork sword, yes," I nod and take a bite. Of my eggs, that is.

"Huh." Bacon takes a second to ponder my impromptu pet name for his penis. "I don't hate it."

He gets lost in my eyes for a moment, and a brilliant smile spreads across his handsome face. I'm pretty sure it mirrors the one on mine.

"Where was I?" he asks.

"You were explaining why you left me with an epic case of lady blue balls."

"Right, right." He laughs. "Alright, so I have no idea how I'm still in this competition because I am internally freaking out every second I'm on that set. And today was even worse than usual since it was our first studio audience."

"Really?" I gnaw on a piece of thick-cut bacon. "You'd never know."

"Even when I'm splattering the host with chocolate sauce because my hands won't stop shaking?"

"Aw, that was nothing," I soothe. "You heard Mairin. She 'never objects to a handsome guy splattering her with sauce.'

Sidebar: isn't it a bit cannibalistic for us to be eating bacon right now?"

"I've endured this pork-centric nickname for over a decade," he says as he holds up his own slice. "Should I also have to suffer through abstaining from eating bacon? We all know bacon is fucking delicious."

"It is indeed." I hold up my slice and tap it to his. "Cheers."

"Oh! That reminds me. How about an evening mimosa? I got the oranges at the Union Square farmers' market. Champagne is from this great little shop on Columbus and Seventy-third. Do you know it?"

"I don't think so." *Because I lied to you, and I don't really live here.* "But a mimosa sounds great, thank you."

He moves to the refrigerator and gets a pitcher of freshly squeezed orange juice. "Anyway, I never considered myself a particularly anxious person, but it turns out, if you put me on a stage or in a spotlight, I'm a mess. I use every ounce of mental and emotional energy I have to get through these tapings, and then I pass out after every single one—whether I like it or not." He pours the juice into two fluted glasses. "That wasn't a problem until I brought a beautiful, hilarious woman home with me, and I crashed right when things were getting good." He grabs a bottle of champagne. "Who am I kidding? Things were good the moment I laid eyes on her, and they only got better from there. Plus, it was pretty adorable that she snuggled up and napped right along with me."

He is the sweetest man.

"Gosh, who is this woman? She sounds fantastic."

"Oh, she is. She's hot as hell too. The second I saw her, my pork sword was like..." He positions the bottle of champagne right at his crotch, and with a loud *pop*, the cork goes flying.

I laugh my ass off. "You're a ridiculous person."

"Is that okay?" He places the glass of juice in my hand and tops it off with champagne.

"More than okay, yeah. I like my guys with a touch of weird."

He smiles as he pours champagne into his own glass. His voice is like melted butter when he cups my cheek and says, "Seriously, I'm sorry I let you down, but I'm hoping you'll forgive me and offer me another chance."

Funny, I'm hoping he'll forgive me and offer me another chance too.

"Nothing to forgive," I avoid his gaze and look down at his kitchen island, where a piece of mail catches my attention. "Who is Harold Hot Man?"

"Who?" Bacon's voice lifts in a tone I haven't heard from him before. He takes our empty plates to the sink.

I abandon my drink and slide off the stool, clutching the bedsheet to my body." Sorry, I didn't mean to snoop. This mail here is addressed to Harold Hot Man. Oh. And it's *from* Harold Hot Man too. Who the heck is Harold Hot Man?"

"Uh, me." He places a champagne glass down in front of me. "And the man who sired me."

"You mean your father?" I ask.

"Nope." He aggressively scrubs our plates. "He doesn't get that title. 'The man who sired me will do.'"

There is obviously a story there. Being brand new to this man's life and having spent the earlier part of the day lying to him, I don't feel like I have the right to pry further into what is clearly a sensitive subject. But I do need to get clarity on one thing.

"Your real name is Harold Hot Man?!"

"Sort of. You're saying it wrong, though. It's Hotman."

"That's what I said. Hot Man."

He chuckles and settles our plates on a dishrack. "It's one word. Think Dustin Hoffman. You wouldn't call him Dustin

Hoff *Man*, would you? He's Dustin Hoffman. And yes, *I* am Harold Hotman."

"And people call you a pork product instead."

"They do indeed."

I shake my head in wonder. "What a world." I turn and finally take in his living space. My eyes nearly bug out of my head at the epic bookcase spanning his entire far wall. "Excuse my language Mr. Hotman, but what the fuck is that?" I hoist the bedsheet around me higher and cross the room to get a better look.

"What? My bookcase?"

"Yeah, your bookcase! If you can call it that! What you have here is a veritable library! Oh my gosh, dude! Eclectic much?"

Bacon joins me and hands me my abandoned mimosa. "You think?"

"Uh, yeah!" I say with a heavy dose of "duh" in my tone. "On this shelf alone you have Nietzsche, Proust, Karin Slaughter, and Danielle Steel."

He shrugs. "I like variety. I assume you're a big reader too?"

"What makes you say that?" I take the glass from him and swiftly scan the shelves.

"Well, you're physically drooling right now…"

I swipe at my chin with the bedsheet.

"Also, it's sort of a prerequisite for your work, right?"

Right. I told him I was in publishing.

That wasn't so much a *lie,* but a wish. A dream, really. One I hadn't vocalized in so long. I've wanted to be a writer since I was a little kid. As soon as I learned to read and form my own words on the page, I filled notebook after notebook with my stories. I shared them with anyone who would listen.

But then my parents died, and I just…stopped.

Years later, I went to college as an English major, thinking I could somehow ease my way into a writing career after graduation, but I could never find the same creative flow I'd found as a child. The words just wouldn't come. So I decided to work with children instead. To surround myself with that joy and wonder I once had.

"Let's toast!" I lift my mimosa, trying to get the subject off me. "To Harold 'Bacon' Hotman, a man who cooks *and* reads."

"That seems a low bar if you ask me. Cooking and reading? Those should be considered basic life functions. Certainly not worthy of a toast."

"Don't sell yourself short, sir. You haven't seen the crop of men women deal with in the dating pool. But, point taken." I pause and come up with a better toast. "To Harold 'Bacon' Hotman. Congratulations on making the top ten, Chef."

We finally clink our glasses together and take a sip.

"May I say you look especially beautiful wrapped in nothing but my bedsheet?" he says softly.

My cheeks heat. "You may. And *you*..." I gesture to his red apron with my glass. "Tell me, do you always cook in the semi-nude?"

"No. I don't." His voice goes soft and rumbly. He steps closer to me, takes the glass out of my hand, and places it on a nearby table. "But I had quite a dilemma."

"Oh no," I breathe. "What was your dilemma?"

Bacon fingers the end of the bedsheet wrapped around me. "See, if I got dressed, I risked you thinking I don't want to continue what we started earlier." He yanks the bedsheet off me. It falls to the floor, leaving me completely naked in front of his bookshelf.

"And you do want to continue?" My voice is husky and deep in response to his touch. He cradles my breasts in his hands and gently squeezes, his thumb grazing a nipple.

"I do," he pulls me against him, his hardness pressing right into my softness. "I want to continue."

I crane my neck as he rains kisses down my throat. I reach

around him and grab the globes of his ass. I consider giving his apron tie a tug but then think better of it.

"Back to my dilemma," he says between passionate kisses. "I didn't want to get dressed, but I did want to cook for you. Bacon—as we know—is hot and shoots grease every which way when it sizzles. I couldn't have my cock out at a cookout and risk a burn, ya know?" He pauses abruptly, doubting his dirty talk. "Not that I was taking my cock *out*, as in outside. 'Cock out at a cookout' just sounded fun."

"It does sound fun," I agree, so aroused now that I'm seconds away from jumping this man. But I'm curious about what would happen if I let him steer this. I want to see where he takes us next.

"You want to do something with me?" he whispers in my ear, his trim beard causing goose bumps to race over my skin as it skims over my jaw.

"I want to do everything with you, Chef."

"Damn woman, it's like you can read my mind."

"What?" I pull back slightly to look him in the eyes. "You want me to call you Chef?"

His eyes light up in boyish wonder, but the erection tenting his apron is all man. "Yeah. I want to take you over my kitchen counter while you call me Chef."

I stand straight, give him a salute, and say, "Yes, Chef."

The salute probably wasn't necessary, but it felt right at the moment. He's certainly not complaining as he leads me the few feet back into the kitchen area and bends me over the marble island.

He goes to remove his apron.

"No, Chef. Keep the apron on." I lock eyes with him over my shoulder.

Bacon beams. "You are the most amazing woman I've ever met."

"Stop talkin' and start cookin', Chef."

"Yes, ma'am."

Earlier, he entered me slowly, sensually. This time, he lifts his apron and drives into me like a man—more specifically, a *chef*—possessed. He stretches me almost to the point of discomfort. But then there's only pleasure.

"Do you like that?" he huffs as we find our rhythm.

"Yes, Chef!" I cry out.

The marble is cool under my belly and breasts. His calloused hands are warm and gripping my hips. With every thrust he makes, his bunched-up red apron scratches my lower back. Somehow, that sensation ratchets up my desire for him. I suddenly wish he was wearing a chef hat, too, to complete the look.

"What you're doing is perfect, Chef. Absolutely perfect," I pant. Each time I call him Chef, he increases his vigor. "I'm just wondering if perhaps you have one of those starchy white chef hats on hand?"

"You know I do." He reaches for a cabinet to the left— never losing contact with me—and the angle shift proves to be glorious. I let out a moan.

"You like that, huh?"

"I do, Chef. I really do!"

"Well then I'm going to stay right here, Chef." He puts on the white hat and grips my hips harder. I wouldn't think it were possible, but he kicks into an even higher gear.

I can barely speak at this point. Somehow, I manage to squeak out, "Wait. *I'm* Chef too?"

"You bet you are, baby. Same team, right? We're in this together."

We're in this together.

Those words melt my heart and skyrocket my guilt. But I try to stay present to what's happening right now. Because at this very moment, this incredible man is making a meal of me, and the temperature is only rising.

He hits just the right spot, and I scream "Yes, Chef! Yes, Chef! Yes, Chef!" as my whole world turns white hot.

He continues to thrust, allowing me to ride out every last wave of pleasure, but he must really like this "Yes, Chef!" stuff, because it's only a moment later when his powerful hips jerk one final time and he finds his own release.

I lie there, still splayed on the counter, not sure I can move. A strong arm reaches under my belly and another under my chest. He lifts me off the cool marble until I'm standing again, my back to his front. His warm hands massage my breasts as he whispers in my ear, "We're not finished here, are we?"

"No, Chef," I exhale. "Not by a long shot."

"Good, because I have plans for you, Chef." He turns me around and kisses me slow and deep.

I can honestly say this is the most fun I've had in my entire life. And it's all thanks to this sexy, amazing man.

That's why It breaks my heart to know I can never see him again.

CHAPTER 7
BACON

Four Months Later…

I'm sitting in Skyline Diner, sipping a cup of coffee, when Trent rushes in, brushing snowflakes off his coat.

"I have something important to tell you." He drops into the booth across from me and pours hot water over the black tea bag already waiting for him.

"You're not canceling tonight, right? I really need you there."

Tonight is the finale of *Yes, Chef,* when the winner is chosen. I can't believe it, but it's all come down to me and another guy. And it's all happening live tonight on national television.

He laughs. "Dude. I missed one taping four months ago, and I've been at every one since, haven't I? Think I can be let off the hook at some point?"

He's right. I gotta let that one go. After all, his absence is the reason I allowed a hilarious, gorgeous woman into my life that day. It's hard to know whether to thank him or curse him for that, though, because that same woman rocked my world one night and destroyed it the following morning when she disappeared without a trace.

"You're thinking about her, huh?" Trent says after a sip of tea.

"How'd you know?" I ask.

"Your face does this thing when you think about her. It gets smooshy."

"Smooshy?"

"Yeah. Relax your forehead, bro. Not a good look for a hot TV star like you."

I scrub my hands over my face to release the tension there. "You said you had something to tell me. What is it?"

"There's been a break in the case," Trent says seriously.

My heart rate picks up. "The Cookie Case?"

He groans. "Do you have to call it 'The Cookie Case'? You make it sound like we're preschool puppy investigators on the hunt for a missing snack instead of two virile men tracking down a sexy woman."

"Preschool puppy investigators? That's very specific. You're not writing children's books now, are you?" I take a bite of my scrambled eggs and wash them down with orange juice.

"Never." He takes another sip of his tea. "Kids are life-ending career blockers. I hung out with my nephew the other day, and he made me read fifteen *Paw Patrol* books. I'll never be the same."

"Wow. Tell me how you really feel." I laugh.

"I'm not like you, buddy. I don't daydream about getting hitched to one woman and filling her with my bacon bits."

"One dream! I had one dream where I had kids and called them my 'Bacon Bits' and you're never going to let me live it down, are you?"

"No, I will not. I will bring it up often. In public and at full volume." Trent waves to a sweet old lady at the table next to us whose mouth is open in apparent shock.

Our server places a ham and cheddar omelet down in

front of Trent. We come here so often that they don't even ask for our order anymore.

"Thanks, Carol," we say in unison before she nods and hurries to her next table.

Trent proceeds to shovel food into his mouth like he hasn't eaten in weeks. "So. You wanna know the information I have on your girl or what?"

My girl.

God, I love the sound of that. I know it's crazy, but for one night, that's really how it felt. She was my girl.

"Yes. Please. Tell me everything. See? I knew you'd find her! You were all, 'Bacon, dude, I only play a private investigator in my books. I can't do it in real life.' But you did it. You found her!"

"First, that was a terrible impression of me. And second, I didn't find her. But I do believe I found her grandma."

"Her grandma?" I ask, confused.

"Yes, her grandma. After all our internet searches and phone calls trying to track down a 'female New Yorker named Cookie who works in publishing' came up short, I decided to return to Exhibit A."

Trent whips the merino wool bra from his briefcase and slaps it on the table.

"Right! She said the bra was hand knit by her grandma!" I say way too loudly.

The older lady at the table next to us huffs in our direction, dumps a pile of coins on her table, and shuffles out of the diner. The gentleman in me wants to follow and apologize to her for our inappropriateness, but the part of me who's desperate to find Cookie stays glued to Trent's every word.

"Exactly. The embroidered letters on this tag were too tattered to read at first. I brought it to my tailor. He's a genius with a suit, so I figured what the hell, maybe he could help. He studied the pattern of the embroidery holes and determined that the original lettering must have been 'With Love, From Baabara."

"Barbara? Her grandmother's name is Barbara?" I ask.

"No," Trent says. "Her grandmother's name is Ethel. The sheep is Baabara."

"Okay, I'm lost. Who was talking about a sheep?"

"I searched for Baabara and… here." Trent slides his phone across the table. "Look at this article I found from 2019."

I read the title out loud. "Rambunctious Sheep Disturbs Flower Festival."

"Go on," Trent says. "Keep reading."

"'Fork Lick residents are up in arms after an incident yesterday afternoon when a local sheep named Baabara Streisand crashed through the town's annual flower festival. The sheep bound through the small outdoor arena, grabbing flowers in her muzzle and spitting them back out at fairgoers continually and with rapid-fire precision, leaving local florists angry and without merchandise. One local resident said, "Screw that sheep! Someone needs to get a handle on - '" I cut myself off. "This is fascinating. But what does this have to do with Cookie?"

"Maybe nothing," Trent says. "But scroll down farther. It says the sheep's owner is named Ethel B. Doesn't give her full last name. This girl of yours said her grandma hand knit the merino wool bra for her, right?" He holds it up and unfurls the faded tag. "This one with a tag that used to say With Love, From Baabara?"

"Right," I say.

"So it wouldn't be completely illogical to assume this Ethel B woman who owns a merino sheep named Baabara could be your girl's grandma."

"Trent, buddy. You're amazing. Now all I need to do is find the grandma, and she can help me find the girl!"

"Whoa, whoa, whoa. Before we get ahead of ourselves…"

Trent puts down his fork, reaches across the table, and takes my hand.

"Um. What the hell, man? Why are you holding my hand?"

Trent draws his hand back like it's on fire. He stabs his fork into his eggs and resumes talking with his mouth full. "Forget it. I just… I have something potentially hurtful to say to you, and my sister says I need to be more sensitive to other people's feelings. I was trying to be kind or whatever."

"By holding my hand?" I scoff.

"I said forget it."

We eat in silence for a few seconds until I break it.

"What's the 'potentially hurtful' thing you need to say?"

He waves me off with his fork.

"We always give it to each other straight. Trent, whatever it is, just say it."

Trent swallows his food and lets out a deep breath. "Look. I love seeing you this excited about a woman. I can't even remember the last time that happened. But…"

"But…?" I try to pull the words out of him.

"Have you considered that she doesn't want to be found?"

My stomach drops. Of course I've considered that.

"What, um. What makes you say that?"

"Oh, I don't know, Bacon. Maybe the fact that she escaped from your bed while you were sleeping? Used a fake name? Lied about where she lives and what she does for a living?" Trent winces. "Sorry. That was sarcastic. My sister also told me I sound like a dick when I lead with sarcasm."

I take a breath, clear my throat, and speak calmly. "She could have had an early meeting the next day and didn't want to disturb me."

"Could've left you a note," he counters.

True.

"And Cookie is probably a nickname," I continue. "That's why we can't find a New Yorker with that name who works in advertising. Also, it was my fault for not getting her last name. And you know what?" It feels like I'm trying to convince myself at this point, but I can't stop coming up with explanations for her absence. "Maybe she wanted to put the ball in my court. I mean, she pursued *me* initially, right? So maybe she wanted me to reciprocate and pursue *her*."

"Without leaving you her real name. Or a way to contact her." Trent squints out the window. We both watch bundled-up tourists trudging by. After a moment of silence, he says, "She spent the night at your place, right?"

"Right."

"So she knows where to find you."

"I suppose so."

He reaches for my hand again. "It's been four months. If she wanted to, she would."

I take one last gulp of my coffee and place some bills on the table. I slide on my coat.

"Come on," Trent protests. You told me to give it to you straight. That's what I did. Now you're gonna leave?"

"Yeah, I am gonna leave. I'm not mad at you. I'm just..." God, I don't know what I am. "Look, I hear what you're saying, and I appreciate the sleuthing you did for me, but... you weren't there that day, Trent. You didn't see our chemistry. What I felt for this girl that day was real. There's a reason—a good reason—she went missing. And I'm going to figure it out."

He shakes his head. "She played you, man. Forget her and move on."

"Fuck that." I grab the woolen bra and clutch it to my chest. "I'll see you at the finale tonight, then I'm catching the first bus out of here tomorrow morning. I have a grandma to find in Fork Lick."

CHAPTER 8
COLLEEN

"Not a fan of that show, huh?" my twin's girlfriend Diane says as we pull out of the driveway of Bedd Fellows Farm. "Every Sunday when your gran turns it on after family dinner, you split."

"What show?"

I know exactly what show she's talking about.

They say mothers have a sixth sense when it comes to their children. Well, the same must be true of grandmothers because immediately after my tryst with one particular hot chef four months ago, Gran decided that her favorite TV show needs to be our family's favorite too. She now insists we watch *Yes, Chef!* after every Sunday dinner, and it's absolute torture for me.

I can't bear seeing Bacon's beautiful face on that screen, knowing he was mine for one perfect day, and I blew it by bailing on him the next morning.

"Colleen. You're acting like that night your sophomore year when you forgot you had a paper due for McGolrick's class. What's going on? What's this errand we're running?"

Diane and I went to Vassar College. We connected as members of Vassar SEED – Students for Equitable Environmental Decisions. We only had one class together, though, and ran in different friend circles, so we weren't especially close back then. I always liked her and wished I knew her better. Fate granted me that wish a few months ago when she and Sam connected through farming business and fell in love. Now, she's the sister I never had. And tonight... she's my unwitting accomplice.

"I'm fine. Everything's fine." I say it to Diane, but it's more a chant for myself.

I pull the car into the Quick Lick parking lot and find a space. There's plenty at this time of night. Most people in this small town are doing the same thing the Bedds are doing right now: gathering their big families around the Sunday night dinner table.

I turn the engine off and stare at the convenience store lit up in the night.

"Um. What are we doing here?" Diane says.

"I, uh, I need you to go in and grab something for me."

"You want me to go into The *Quick* Lick with you?" Her voice rises in pitch. "Quick as in Ginny Quick?"

"Oh god. Right. I forgot." I sigh and rest my forehead on the steering wheel. Hunching forward like this makes my pants feel even tighter than they did a minute ago. And that's not due to the roasted chicken legs, caramelized sweet potatoes, string beans, and homemade sourdough bread with salted butter that I ate at dinner. I had to excuse myself while doing the dishes and pray to the porcelain god. A few weeks ago, I thought I had a nasty stomach bug, but clearly, I was wrong. Stomach bugs might cause a girl to puke, but generally, they don't cause the girl a ten-pound weight gain while simultaneously setting her nipples ablaze.

"You forgot," Diane repeats back to me, incredulous. "You forgot that Ginny single-handedly tried to shame me to all of Fork Lick and steal my boyfriend at the same time. And this Scuttlebutt 'newspaper' thing she's doing? It's ridiculous."

"No. I mean, yeah. I'm sorry, I've been... distracted lately."

"No kidding. Sam's twin sense is firing on all cylinders. Colleen, he's really worried. Could you put him out of his misery at some point and tell him what the heck is going on with you?"

Sam can drive me buggy sometimes, but my connection with him means the world to me. One of my biggest fears after our parents died was that I'd lose him someday too when he found "his person." Diane is exactly the kind of girl I always hoped he'd find. She loves Sam, accepts him completely, and celebrates all his quirks. They're building a beautiful life together, and she never makes us feel bad about the intensity of our twinship.

Come to think of it, the Bedd family has been welcoming lots of new female energy into our fold lately. Lia was Ethan's "the one who got away," but after some bumps in the road this year, he got her back. Seeing how that serious dude softens every time he looks at her is adorable. Alex is a changed man too. Molly's open heart and adventurous spirit perfectly balance his reserved nature.

Look at everyone finding love. I should get on the phone with my little brother Jackson and commiserate about our lack of luck in that arena. Actually, scratch that. The man is a rock star. He likely has women crawling all over him in LA.

Diane clears her throat, jolting me out of my reverie.

"Oh. Sorry. You're waiting for an answer."

Diane cocks her head and continues to wait.

"Yes," I say. "I will talk to Sam. But the nature of what I need to tell him depends on the results of us going into that store."

"Cryptic much?" She laughs, but I can tell she's getting exasperated with me.

"I was going to ask you to go in there for me, but obviously, I can't send you into the Ginny lion's den alone. Can we go in together?"

"You're freaking me out, but yes. Of course. Whatever you need." She pats my hand and sends me a soft smile.

My eyes well. "Have I told you lately I'm really glad you fell in love with my brother?"

"You have." She gives me another pat and reaches for her door handle. "Let's get this over with. Whatever it is."

We walk through the doors hand in hand. As usual, Ginny is quick to leap upon her victims, er, customers.

"Hello, ladies!" she calls from the cashier stand.

"Hey Gin," I say as neutrally as possible and attempt to drag Diane down the first aisle with me.

"Could I have a word with Diane?" Ginny says, hot on our heels.

Diane stops and faces her. "I don't know, Ginny. During our short acquaintance, I've learned that your words tend to be hurtful and often untrue."

"I'm turning over a new leaf." Ginny looks and sounds sincere when she says it. "I'm embarrassed by the drama I've caused. To you, Diane. And to the Bedd family in general. And all because I couldn't get over some guy. Isn't that silly?"

She laughs.

We don't.

At our silence, Ginny continues, "I don't expect bygones to be bygones right away. But I do owe you an apology, so I'm sorry."

I narrow my eyes at her. "I'll be honest, Gin, I'm not sure what to make of this. To what do we owe this sudden self-reflection and empathy?"

"My *Scuttlebutt* publication is a flop. For months, I've received daily 'letters to the editor' telling me to *butt* out of Fork Lickers' business, or they'll *scuttle* me out of town. Everywhere I go, I'm confronted by someone I've hurt or humiliated." She sighs. "I don't want to be the girl people love to hate anymore. I'd much prefer to be a girl someone actually loves one day. At the very least, I'd like to be a girl who has friends, you know? Not that I know what that feels like, but I'd like to experience a real relationship at some point. Anyway, I'm realizing that in order for that to happen, I need to stop being such a nosy, judgmental, gossiping biatch."

"Sounds like a good first step," I say, my eyes darting toward the aisle I desperately need to visit.

Ginny actually picks up on my cue and says sadly, "Alright, thanks for hearing what I had to say, ladies. I'll leave you to your shopping now. Meet you at the front when you're ready to check out."

When she's out of earshot, Diane whispers, "That was so sad! Is it bizarre that I feel bad for her?"

I shrug. "Everyone deserves a second chance, I guess."

"I'm going to talk to her. Go get what you need, and I'll meet you up front?"

That's actually the perfect plan.

We part ways, and I head to that same aisle where I got caught staring at condoms all those months ago. Perhaps I should've stared a little harder, and I wouldn't be in this mess right now?

Today, a different tiny box is calling my name. I grab it and boldly march to the front of the store. I have a plan, and it's a good one.

When I reach the cashier stand, Diane and Ginny are chatting and laughing like old pals.

This is it. This is my chance.

"Here you go, Diane!" I chirp. "I found what you were looking for!"

I place a pregnancy test on the cashier's belt. It lands directly between Diane and Ginny. Both their mouths drop open wide, then two sets of eyes swing to me.

My only response is a tight smile and the pounding of my heart.

Ginny's voice is strained when she speaks. "Diane, have you been implanted with Samuel's seed?"

A wave of nausea rolls through my stomach. "Ginny? Gross. That's my brother you're talking about."

"I'm not talking to you, Colleen!" Ginny snaps. She may be turning over a new leaf, but change takes time, and this "news" is understandably rocking her world right now. She repeats with eerie calm, "Diane, have you been implanted with Samuel's seed?"

Diane continues to stare at me, her eyes even wider now. I silently plead with her to please, please, please go along with this.

She takes a deep breath and instantly becomes my hero. "With the amount of seed-spewing activity we've been engaged in lately, Ginny, my guess is yes. My guess is there is Samuel Spawn implanting in my uterine wall at this very moment."

Yeah, I'm gonna barf.

"At this very moment?" Ginny squeaks.

Diane continues in a spectacularly heinous fashion. "Yes, Ginny. Just now we were all gathered for a big Bedd family Sunday dinner. Everyone was there. I'm telling you *everyone*, Ginny. His gran, his sister, his brothers, their girlfriends... I locked eyes with Samuel across the table. He was looking so juicy and virile. My mouth was watering. My panties were soaked. His expression told me that he was as hard as the oak table we were all gathered around. And god help me, Ginny, at that moment, I had to have him, even with his grandmother sitting beside me."

"You made love in front of Mrs. Bedd?" Ginny's eyes widen to saucers.

"Of course not," Diane says coolly. "We excused ourselves,

rushed out to the barn, and literally rolled in the hay. Over and over and over and over and over and over..."

"Alright, Diane," I whisper. "I think that'll do."

"Wasn't that itchy?" Ginny marvels, almost impressed.

"It was, Ginny!" Diane nods with seriousness. "It was very itchy. But Samuel's cock is always worth it."

She just mentioned my brother's name and the word cock in the same sentence.

This is not going to end well for me.

Ginny gets unexpectedly practical and helpful. "You know you can't tell if you're pregnant immediately after intercourse, Diane."

"Oh, I know, Ginny." Diane smiles sweetly. "But the fact is, Samuel's sperm swims through me on a daily basis. Over the past month, there have been *many* opportunities for a drop of Sam Pearl Jam to start a beautiful ruckus in my uterus."

That did it.

In the nick of time, I grab a paper bag meant for groceries and empty the contents of my stomach into it.

Ginny is still, eyes darting between Diane and me.

I slap a twenty-dollar bill in Ginny's palm, grab the test in one hand, my bag of barf in the other, and hightail it to the door, shouting, "Nice to see you, Gin! Good luck with the new leaf!" as I go.

A second after I slam the door and settle into the driver's seat, Diane enters the vehicle and sits beside me. Seems she's waiting for me to speak first.

I finally form words. "That. Was. Heinous."

"I know!" Diane cringes. "Good thing you have quick reflexes and got the bag in time, though!"

"I'm referencing the *verbal* vomit that came out of your mouth!" I turn on the engine and pull onto the street. "Geez, Diane. That is my brother you were talking about. I think my ears are still bleeding."

"I got the focus off you, didn't I?"

I shudder. "You certainly did."

We drive in silence for the few minutes it takes to reach the farm. I turn off the engine but make no move to exit the car.

"So? What's the deal?" she says softly. "You're pregnant?"

"I don't know," I sigh. "Maybe? Probably not? I don't know. My period has always been irregular, so I didn't even notice I skipped the past three until now. I've put on weight I can't explain. And I've been feeling really nauseous lately too, so..."

"So maybe the puking incident wasn't my fault?" Diane says hopefully.

"No, it was definitely your fault! 'Samuel Spawn'? 'Sam Pearl Jam'? Really?"

She places a hand over mine on the console. "Never again, I promise. I appreciated Ginny's apology, and I'll work on forgiving her, but you can't blame me for getting a little saucy and staking my claim after everything she's done, can you?"

"I suppose not, but still. Bleh."

I turn the small box over in my hands and look up at the house, all lit up. Shadowy figures of my family move behind the gauzy curtains. Faint laughter seeps out through the front window that we always leave open a crack.

"Who's the guy?" Diane asks.

I fight the tears that want to form. "What guy?"

"Usually, when someone thinks they might be pregnant, a guy was involved at some point?"

I shrug. "No one special."

Nothing could be further from the truth. He was special. He *is* special. And I know it was just one night, but I miss him. All I wanted was one night to be wild with no strings attached. So why did the guy I chose have to be so kind and adorable and unforgettable?

His words come back to haunt me like they have every day for the last four months.

I hate lies. Please don't lie to me.

What do you say to that after you'd already lied to a man all day? For fun? I did what he asked. I promised not to lie to him from that point on. But the damage had already been done.

"Well," Diane says. "Should we go inside?"

"You can. I'm..." Another peal of laughter rings from inside the house. "I think I'm going to stay out here for a bit. Don't worry. I'll be in soon."

Diane reaches her hand out. "Want me to toss that bag for you?"

"What a pal," I joke as I hand over the paper bag full of my regurgitated dinner. "Thanks, Diane. Sorry if I just started a rumor that you're pregnant. Though Ginny did seem sincere that her gossip rag days are behind her."

"I guess we'll see." She steps out of the car, but before she closes the door, she dips her head back inside. "Colleen?"

"Yeah?" I swipe a tear from my cheek that I hadn't even realized had fallen.

"Whatever news you get and whatever you decide, you have a whole support system ready to lift you up. You're strong. Your family loves you. I promise you're going to be fine."

"Thanks." My voice is a near whisper.

The moment Diane disappears into the house, I burst into tears.

CHAPTER 9
BACON

I'M BACKSTAGE GETTING MY MAKEUP TOUCHED UP DURING A commercial break. Yep, I wear makeup now. When I'm on TV, at least.

"You're awfully quiet," Kara, our makeup artist, says. "Nervous about the big finale moment? For what it's worth, I'm betting on you, buddy. I don't think you have anything to worry about."

The funny thing is, for the first time ever, I'm not worried about this show. In fact, I'm not even thinking about the show. In less than thirty minutes, I could be the recipient of an enormous amount of money to fund my own restaurant anywhere in the continental United States, but the only thing on my mind is getting this finale over with so I can catch a bus to Fork Lick and find my girl.

I can't get into all that right now, though, so I just shrug and say, "Eh."

"Eh?" Kara laughs. "We just got word that over nine million viewers are tuning in live tonight, and all you have to say is 'eh'?"

I shrug again.

"Okay, you've got to stop shrugging while I do your makeup."

I relax my shoulders. "Sorry. You're right. This is all really exciting, and normally, I would be nervous, but my mind is on other things, I guess."

"Teach me your ways, sir. I'd be shaking in my boots!" She applies a light mist to my face as the finishing touch, then whips off the drape that was protecting my white chef coat. "Alright, big guy. You are good to go."

"Thanks, Kara." I hop out of the makeup chair and head back to my cooking station, where my final creation simmers on the stove.

Our stage manager April approaches with a big smile. "I was about to tell you places in five, but here you are, ready to go."

"Here I am." I smile back at her.

"Someone has a secret," she singsongs. "What's up? Gimme the scoop!"

She and I have gotten close over the past few months. She regales me with stories about the lesbian dating scene in the city, and more than once, I've bored her while recounting the details of my one and only night with my dream girl.

"There's been a break in the Cookie Case," I say.

April squeals. "Yes, yes, yes! Ah, I'm so relieved. You don't know how much it's pained me that I couldn't just go into our audience records and get you more information on her. I mean, I'm sure that even snagging her last name would have done wonders."

"Rules are rules, and I get it. We can't have horny TV chefs accessing audience email addresses to procure hot dates, can we? Privacy policies are in place for a reason," I say. And I mean it. But I'd be lying if I said there weren't moments over the past few months when I cursed my morals and fantasized about hiring someone to hack into that system to solve this mystery for good.

She checks her watch. "Alright. We officially have four

minutes until showtime. Hit me with the deets, and hit me with them fast!"

I quickly review all the information Cookie gave me about herself that day. I tell her the intel Trent uncovered about Cookie's potential grandmother in Fork Lick, and I lay out my plan to travel upstate tomorrow to finally put the last pieces of this puzzle together.

April's eyebrows furrow. "Wait a second. You said she's in publishing?"

"Yeah. She never got specific about what aspect of publishing, but yes."

"Huh." April speaks into her headset. "Three minutes to places."

"What's 'huh'?" I ask as I straighten my chef's hat and secure my apron. "What does 'huh' mean?"

"She was at the August twentieth show, right? I only remember the date because it was my birthday that day."

"Happy belated birthday, April!" I hold out my hand for a fist bump.

She chuckles. "It was four months ago, Bacon. I think we're past the need for birthday wishes."

"Well, I'm sorry I missed it." I shake my fist, still waiting for that bump.

She taps her knuckles to mine. "You're too nice for your own good. Has anyone ever told you that?"

Too many times to count.

"I hate to break it to you, bud, but I think she was untruthful about a few things."

"What do you mean?"

"That week, we were saluting schoolteachers across America. Every single audience member that day was verified as a public elementary school teacher. And they were all from the tri-state area. Not New York City proper. You don't remember all Mairin's little speeches on camera that day about the wonderful work teachers do?"

"April, I'm so nervous during those shows. I barely register anything anyone says."

"Right. Well, whoever your mystery girl is, she must be a teacher." She places a hand on my shoulder. "I'm sorry to say this, bud. But if they lie about basic things like where they live and what they do for a living, there's a good chance they lie about more important stuff too, like relationships and marital status. I'm with your friend Trent here, Bacon. I think you need to move on from this one."

I stand there in silence.

She looked me right in the eyes and promised not to lie.

"Can I ask you something?" April says carefully. "What's so special about this girl?"

"We, uh…" I clear my throat. "We just really—I mean, I *thought* we connected. She was funny and free and—"

"The sex was phenomenal, right?" She shakes her head in disappointment for me. "That's how they get ya."

The sex *was* phenomenal. But that was like the icing on the cake. I felt steady with her. Everything just felt… right.

"Have you ever felt more like yourself when you're with someone?" I ask quietly.

"Oh, buddy." She sighs. "I'm sorry. But, hey, it's…" She checks the time again. "One minute to places. You've worked hard for this. Shake this off for now and get out there and win this thing! We'll talk more later."

She takes her spot in the tech booth. I take mine at the stove. But before I power my phone down and the lights come up, I have to check something. I open my search engine and type in "Fork Lick elementary schools." If her grandmother lives there, it's not absurd to assume she might too.

It's apparently a very small town, so I only get one hit. I pull up Fork Lick Elementary's official website. It's rudimentary at best, but they do have a staff page full of smiling teacher photos along with their bios.

There she is.

The woman I've been fantasizing about for four months.

She's as bright and beautiful as ever, but that's where the similarities end.

Colleen Bedd
Kindergarten Teacher

My name is Colleen Bedd. I am a lifelong Fork Lick resident. This is my seventh year teaching at FLE, and I love it. My favorite thing about teaching kindergarten is watching kiddos learn to read. It's like an amazing magic trick that I get to see every day. My superpower is having a book recommendation for every mood. Fork Lick Elementary kiddos are always welcome to borrow stories from my shelf! Just give a knock on Room 101. My idea of a perfect day is taking an adventurous day trip to visit New York City. Here's to hoping we all have a fantastic year!

Well, she had an adventurous day in New York City alright.

I guess that's all I was to her: a quick trip. She never had any intention of exploring more. She couldn't even be bothered giving me her real name.

Maybe some guys wouldn't be bothered by this. They might even get off on the idea that a woman wove a false story and used them for a day. But when you grow up with a father whose entire life was a lie, your tolerance for untruths is low, nonexistent even.

"Places, everyone." April's voice comes over the loudspeaker.

I do one more thing before I power down my phone.

I open the MTA app for trains and buses leaving Manhattan and cancel my trip to Fork Lick tomorrow morning.

Colleen Bedd? I'm done with you.

CHAPTER 10
COLLEEN

AFTER A GOOD CRY SESSION, I FINALLY GET OUT OF MY CAR, TINY box in hand. I know I should go in the house and enjoy dessert with my family—I really missed these Sunday dinners when they petered out, and I'm thrilled by their resurgence—but I can't be surrounded by all that energy right now. Whatever the outcome of this test, I need to process it alone.

Or perhaps with a really cool sheep.

Call her coddled. Call her out of control. But over the years, I've come to call her my confidant.

I make my way over to Baabara's pen and find her in a rare moment of repose. "Pen" isn't exactly accurate, though. A palace is more like it. Now that I think about it, this sheep sister of mine has more space than I do in my tiny childhood room in Gran's house.

A few years ago, I finally struck out on my own and got a small studio apartment in town. I told everyone it was awesome. I asserted to anyone who'd listen that I was thrilled to be on my own. But the truth was, I struggled. Big time. Here's the thing about big families: they're so loud, you can't think. It wasn't until I was all alone in my little bachelorette pad that I realized I'd come to depend on that noise. Because when it gets quiet enough, you know what happens?

You start to hear yourself. That little voice in your head that tells you something has to change. That you're not living your life as fully and authentically as you can. That voice whispered to me at first and got louder by the day until I couldn't stand it anymore. So, when Grandad passed, I acted like I was taking one for the team by moving back to Bedd Fellows Farm to care for Gran. But the reality is, I was relieved. Because that wily old woman has always taken care of *me*.

And right now, I can't bring myself to face her.

"Hey girl, hey." I give Baabara my usual greeting when I need to talk. She looks up at me but doesn't deign to saunter over. I go to her instead and sit down beside her. "I know Jackson is your favorite, but do you think you have a few minutes to hang with little ole me? Oh, don't give me that look. We all know it's true." Baabara lets out a sad bleat. "I know, girl. I miss him too. But he's on tour now, living his dream. Hopefully, we'll see him again soon."

Baabara nudges the small box in my hand. "'What's that,' you ask. Oh nothing. Just a little test that will determine the course of the rest of my life. No biggie." A cold wind brushes my cheek and reminds me how absurd what I'm about to do really is.

"Here's the deal, Baabs—"

Baabara snuffs at me.

"Sorry. I know you hate that nickname. I don't love when the guys call me Collie either. If it makes you feel any better, people say that having nicknames is a sign you are loved."

Baabara's not buying it.

"Fine. I'll go easy on the 'Baabs' from here on out. Here's the deal," I say again as I tear open the box and pull out the test. "I need to pee on this stick. I can't do it inside the house with our crazy family around. Sam's twin sense will go wild the second I enter the bathroom, and I won't have a moment to myself to process. So, I thought maybe you could be my sidekick for this operation. You pee outside, right? How hard can it be?" She snuffs at me again. "No offense."

Baabara turns her back on me and wanders to the entrance of her enclosure.

"Good idea, good! You stay on the lookout and let me know if anyone's coming."

I take the cap off the blue plastic contraption. "I will simply pull down my pants... pop a little squat here, and... pee on this stick! Haha! I did it!" Another breeze whips past. "Dammit, it's cold out here. We need to get you some space heaters, girl!"

I re-cap the test and place it on the ground next to me. I'm about to pull my pants back up when I realize the gap in my plan. "Hey, Baabs—I mean, Baabara, you don't happen to have tissues or toilet paper out here, do ya?" With the way my grandmother coddles this animal, it wouldn't surprise me. I scan the enclosure, and the only thing that could sorrrrrrt of solve my problem... is hay.

"A girl's gotta do what a girl's gotta do." I grab a handful of hay and dab as best as I can. I'm applying hand sanitizer from my purse right as a loud burst of laughter spills from the house. Ugh. They're still watching that show. But wait. Why would their voices be so loud unless...

"Oh my god, the door is open!" I say out loud. I realize my mistake before the words fully exit my mouth.

In a move that proves Baabara truly does understand English, she skitters a few feet toward the farmhouse.

"Baabara, no!" I scold. In a surprise maneuver, she shuffles the few feet back to me, almost like she's weighing the decision on whether to be a good sheep or a bad sheep.

She decides to be the *worst* sheep.

Baabara seizes the little blue test in her teeth and hauls sheep ass to the front door.

"Baarbara, no!" I shout again, more desperate this time. I try to chase her but trip over the jeans still around my ankles.

By the time I pull them up, Baabara is already nudging open the flimsy aluminum storm door.

"SHEEP!" my brother Ethan bellows from inside the house. I'd know his disapproving wail anywhere. This isn't the first time Baabara has barged her way into the house. And it likely won't be the last. But as far as I know, it *is* the first time she's brandished a weapon of sorts.

I fly into the house, literally on her tail, but the sheep won't be deterred. She's bouncing off furniture, running through people's legs and generally creating as much mayhem as possible.

"Someone didn't tug the door until it clicked!" Alex accuses the room. "How many times do we have to say it? You must tug the door until it clicks!"

"Was it me? Oh my gosh, I think it was me!" Diane shouts guiltily. "I'm sorry, I didn't know I had to tug the door until it clicked!"

"It's okay, sweetheart," Sam says and wraps an arm around her, shielding her not only from the sheep but also my older brothers' wrath. They hate when Baabara gets in the house.

"No, Sam. It's not okay!" Ethan yells while trying to outmaneuver the animal and corner her. She eludes him every time.

I faintly register that *Yes, Chef!* is still blaring from the TV screen. As usual, I avoid looking at Bacon. It hurts too much.

Cool as a cucumber, Gran rises from the sofa and says, "Boys. Baabara is feeding off your energy. If you calm down, she'll calm down. And Ethan? Apologize to Diane this instant. She's new to the family and made an honest mistake."

Ethan sighs. "My apologies, Diane. There are only so many times I can tolerate this wooly mammoth shitting on my shoes."

"Understood." Diane nods.

Baabara continues to ricochet through the living room. She

veers dangerously close to Gran's china cabinet, but Lia and Molly join hands just in time, creating a two-person human barricade. They start a gentle chorus of "Shh, shh, shh, shh," which calms the sheep immediately and saves a century of Bedd family china from crashing to the floor.

"Well done, Lia and Molly," Gran praises softly. "See, boys?" She turns a sharp eye to Ethan and Alex. "Notice how cool and calm your paramours stayed in the face of a would-be crisis? All while you two ran around like chickens with their heads cut off." She sighs and shakes her head. "If you want something done, ask a woman."

My grandmother gets settled in her favorite chair and turns up the volume on the TV. Baabara curls up at her feet like a pet dog. "Gather 'round, everyone! This is a big night on my show. They're announcing the winner any minute. Oh, I really hope it's my sexy Bacon boy."

"Your sexy Bacon boy?" I squeak.

Sam laughs. "Yeah, Gran has it bad for the one with the beard."

I fight the new wave of nausea threatening to overtake me. I've thrown up enough today. Surely, it can't happen again? All I know is I need to get out of here asap, and I've gotta take that pregnancy-test-stealing sheep with me.

I tap my grandmother lightly on the shoulder. "Gran? I'll get Baabara settled outside."

"Oh, it's you," she says with a touch of passive aggression. "Since when do you slip out unannounced while we're doing dishes, missy?"

"Sorry about that, ma'am. I'll do extra dishes next time. I just noticed we were low on milk, and I know you like a splash of milk with your tea, so…"

"So you ran to The Quick Lick?" Sam says, confused.

I look at Diane, who winces and whispers, "Was I not supposed to tell them we went to The Quick Lick?"

Alex chimes in, "Yeah, why the hell would you go to The

Quick Lick for milk when your brother owns a damn creamery?"

"Language, Alex," Gran scolds, then looks at me to answer his question. In fact, the entire family stops and stares.

"I, uh—That's a good question. Hm. I'm not sure how to—"

Then Molly saves me and destroys me with one question. "Is there something in Baabara's mouth?"

Baabara bolts away from Gran's feet, but we're ready for her this time. Taking a lesson from Lia and Molly's approach a few minutes ago, we all hold hands and form a tight circle around the sheep. She's caught with nowhere to go.

"What does she have?" Samuel squints at the sheep.

"Is it a marker?" Lia asks.

Alex guesses, "A thermometer maybe?"

"Baabara?" Gran says sternly. "Drop. Now."

Never one to disobey Gran, Baabara instantly responds by dropping the test.

Face up.

In the middle of the carpet.

With the word "Pregnant" lit up clearly on the tiny digital screen.

Oh my god, I'm pregnant.

A hush falls over the room.

Her work here done, Baabara peacefully saunters to the still-open front door and sees herself out.

"Whose positive pregnancy test is that?" Gran clutches her hands to her heart. "Lia and Ethan?"

Lia shakes her head.

"Not us. Not yet anyway," Ethan says and gives Lia a squeeze.

Gran turns to her second oldest grandchild. "Alex? Is it you and Molly?"

"No, ma'am," Alex says.

Molly echoes him with another, "No, ma'am."

Gran turns to the next obvious choice. "Diane and Samuel?"

Diane's eyes quickly dart to me, then refocus on my grandmother. "I did hear a rumor recently that I was pregnant, so yeah, maybe it's me!"

"Thank you, Diane," I say quietly. "But that won't be necessary."

"Oh my god." Sam locks eyes with me and whispers, "It's you."

"Who's who?" Gran says, her head whipping left and right. "What's who?"

"*Me* who," I say. "I'm the one who's pregnant." I pick up the test so I can look at it more closely, then place it on the coffee table and promptly flop down on the couch.

"Well, how in the world did that happen?"

"Sex, Gran," I sink deeper into the cushions and cover my eyes. "Typically, pregnancy is the result of sex."

Gran huffs. "You think I'm in the dark about sex, missy? I'll have you know that in our twenties, your grandfather and I were quite the exhibitionists. One time, after hours at the county fair, we got on the back of Old Man Tiddy's tractor, and when your grandaddy was good and ready, he pounded—"

Ethan places a hand on Gran's shoulder. "I am so sorry to interrupt you, Gran, but I really can't handle hearing you complete that sentence."

"I was simply going to say your grandfather pounded the tractor hood and got the engine working again," she says matter-of-factly.

"Oh, thank god," my brothers collectively sigh.

Gran continues, "But *after* that, he made gentle yet vigorous love to me under the moonlight."

For the first time today… I laugh. Once I start, I can't stop. I laugh, and I laugh, and I laugh. Before I know it, I'm in full hysterics.

"Are you, uh… Are you okay?" Alex asks.

"I'm great! Terrific! You gotta hand it to me! When I do something, I really do it, don't I? I set out to be wild for one day. Well, what's wilder than getting knocked up the first time you attempt a one-night stand?"

In a show of sisterly solidarity, Lia, Molly, and Diane surround me on the couch. I rest my head on Molly's shoulder.

Gran sinks into her favorite chair as well and stares into the distance, trying to process this new development, I'm sure. However, my brothers remain standing, like they're ready to march into battle for me.

Ethan clears his throat. Then he clears his throat again. "I'm trying to stay calm and not get all 'big brothery' here. But, uh— I think I can speak for all three of us when I say—"

"Who the hell is the father?" Alex asks for him.

At that moment, music swells from the television, and we turn in unison.

It feels like everything goes into slow motion, and I'm hovering above my body, watching it all happen.

Bacon is crowned the winner of *Yes, Chef!* Season One. Confetti flutters all around him. The producers present him with a check that has more zeros than I've ever seen in my whole life. I know I'm imagining it, but when he looks directly into the camera, I swear he's staring straight into my soul.

"That 'sexy Bacon boy' right there," I say, pointing at the screen. "Harold Hotman is the father."

CHAPTER 11
COLLEEN

The next morning, a note slides under my bedroom door saying:

> *Bedd Family Meeting*
> *Time: Eight a.m. sharp.*
> *Location: Gran's Kitchen*
> *Topic: Colleen's Condition*

Dear lord, they've called a breakfast meeting. Or more specifically, Ethan called a breakfast meeting. I'd know his chicken scrawl handwriting anywhere. He's also the only one old-fashioned enough to call my pregnancy a "condition." He'll get an earful about that from me later.

After the news broke last night, there were lots of "I still don't understand how *Colleen* could be pregnant!" and "Last I checked, Colleen doesn't even date!" I nipped the chaos right in the bud and locked myself in my room for the night, telling them this was my business, and I'd deal with it myself. That didn't stop them from whispering and conspiring in the kitchen for a full hour after I made my dramatic exit. They should know by now that sound travels in this house.

I take my time showering and dressing and purposely

arrive five minutes late to this so-called family meeting. When I enter the kitchen, Gran and my brothers are already seated at the table, totally silent.

"You all stopped talking as soon as you heard me coming," I say, hovering above the empty seat meant for me.

"No, we didn't!" they say in unison, seeming to surprise themselves. Then Ethan purposefully lifts a hand like he's signaling an orchestra, and they all say, "Sit. Eat." Their plastered-on smiles and singsongy voices freak me out.

I scan the table. Our usual morning fare of buttered toast, fried eggs, and glasses of orange juice are at the ready. But something is off.

"Is there a reason no one is drinking coffee? What's with all the herbal tea?"

Gran raises and lowers the tea bag in her cup. "The Bedd boys all love herbal tea, don't they?" she says, using a teaching voice that I know all too well.

Ethan, Alex, and Samuel respond by raising and lowering their own tea bags and saying, "Mmm, yes. Teeeeeeea."

Gran continues. "Pregnant women shouldn't consume caffeine, so as our first show of support, we decided to join you in drinking red raspberry leaf tea. It strengthens the uterine muscles and softens the cervix."

Ethan winces as he takes a sip. "Like we said, mmmmm."

"Actually, guys?" Sam holds up his phone, showing an article about herbal teas. "We don't want to start softening the cervix until thirty-seven weeks."

"Alright, Colleen," Gran says. "You stick to the orange juice for now, then. We'll find you a cervix-friendly tea bag soon."

I slide into my chair, take a big gulp of orange juice, and set the cup down a bit too roughly. "So did you guys rehearse this intervention, or what?"

"Just the 'Sit. Eat.' part," Sam says. "And the 'mmm, yes,

teeeeea' part. But from here on, the discussion will be entirely improvisational."

I give Sam a nod and a tight smile. No matter how bad things get, at least I can always count on my twin to tell me the truth. He's as straightforward as he is sincere.

"Where are your soon-to-be wives?" I ask. "They didn't want to enjoy the show?"

"We thought it would be best if it were the original Bedd family members for this initial meeting," Ethan says, his ice-blue eyes looking even more serious than usual.

"Well, then we ought to call Jackson up while we're at it," I joke.

"We did, actually," Alex says, pointing at the phone propped against the salt and pepper shakers. "He's on video."

Sure enough, my younger brother's handsome face smiles back at me in real time. "Hey, Sis. Congratulations! Or actually—are we saying congratulations? Is 'I heard the news' better at this point?"

I ignore his question and ask one of my own. "Dude, why did you agree to this? Isn't it the crack of dawn in LA?"

"It is, but don't worry. Rock stars are known for staying up late."

Alex rolls his eyes at that. Gran catches him and scolds him with her stare. "Thanks for being here, Jackson," he amends and smooths his dark beard. "We appreciate it."

Another moment of silence descends.

"Well, let's get this over with," I say. "And Ethan, don't think I didn't catch it when you said this is our *initial* meeting on this subject. It is not our initial meeting. It is our only meeting. I appreciate your concern, but I think you all forget I am a twenty-nine-year-old woman. I'm not the same little ten-year-old girl who cried at night unless she was snuggled up in her twin brother's bed—"

"Yeah, now she snuggles up in reality TV stars' beds,"

Alex says under his breath, staring at a square on his signature flannel shirt.

"Alex…" Gran warns at the same time I say, "One reality star! One time! And I'm a grown-ass woman! If I want to sleep with every reality star on planet Earth, it's my prerogative to do so!"

Sam gives me a look. "Wow, pregnancy has really changed you."

He and I instantly devolve into a fit of giggles.

"Anyone know what they're laughing about?" Jackson asks from the video call.

"Never did, never will," Ethan says.

It's one of many private jokes Sam and I have. I don't even know how or why it started, but whenever one of us tries something new or accomplishes something cool, we joke about that person suddenly being "too good" for everyone around them. Like when he learned to ride a two-wheeler before I did, I hit him with a "Wow, bike riding has really changed you." When I was salutatorian at our high school graduation, he made sure to say, "Wow, that smart people award has really changed you."

It's a dumb joke when you try to explain it to other people, but it's our joke, and I love it. The fact that he's busting it out now feels like his way of suggesting that maybe this pregnancy could be a good thing. Perhaps it could change me in a good way.

When I recover from our twin laughing fit, I clear my throat and continue. "As I was saying, this is the only time I am participating in this Bedd family town hall you've orchestrated. I'm sure you have questions. Go ahead. Get them all out of your system."

Alex raises his hand like he's in a classroom. "Here's what I don't understand. You're how many months pregnant now?"

"Around four months," I say.

"Right. Four months. How have you missed the signs for four months?" Alex says, and it feels all sorts of condescending to my ears.

"Yeah, I've been wondering that too," Ethan says.

"Me too," Sam chimes in.

"Actually, me too." Jackson says through the phone, his green eyes narrowing.

"Well," I stretch out the word for added sarcasm. "Since you're all so curious about my reproductive system…"

"Whoa, whoa, whoa, nobody said *that*." Alex puts his fork down with a clank.

"Nonono, please, brothers, let me give you the full details that you're all desiring so deeply."

I may as well have fun with this.

"See, I've always had an irregular menstrual cycle, guys."

Ethan chokes on a bite of toast.

"That must be hereditary," Gran says. "Your mother was the same way."

"Was she?" I give my grandmother my full attention. "Wow. I didn't know that."

It's probably strange for something like that to make me feel closer to my mom, but it does. At one point, she was very much alive, like me, and she experienced some of the same ups and downs that living in a body can bring. Bodies can be bizarre. And they can be beautiful. Miraculous even. Like how is it possible that without my knowledge, my body has been forming a *baby* inside me these past few months?

Back to disturbing my brothers.

"Crazy, right, guys? Yeah, some months I just have real light spotting. Cute little red speckles. That's it! Other months, though? It's like a slasher movie down there! Just days and days of nonstop bleeding."

"Please make her stop," Alex says to Gran.

"No way!" I say. "You want to be informed, right? I mean, isn't that why you all called this meeting? So yeah, these past few months were of the spotting and speckling variety. Or so I thought. Looks like I skipped three periods entirely. But I barely noticed with all the financial stress at the farm. You may not know this, but stress can affect menstruation. However, I *did* notice my breasts were consistently sore—which can be a sign of pregnancy. But honestly, when you're rocking double Ds on a tiny frame like I am, your breasts and back are kind of always sore. In hindsight, though, my nipples were unusually tight and tingly and—"

"Point made!" Ethan says, exasperated. "We don't need all the details."

"You sure?" I ask sweetly. "Because I thought maybe I'd explain all the positions the reality star and I did that night too if you're interested. They do say certain positions are more conducive to conceiving. Angles matter, apparently. And we tried quite a few. If I had to choose, I'd say my favorite one was—"

"Alright, guys!" Alex takes a last swig of his orange juice and stands up. "Are we doing this or what?"

Uh-oh. I think my impromptu plan may be backfiring.

Ethan rises from the table. "Hell yeah, we're doing this. Sam?"

"I'm in. Jackson?"

"Yeah. I'm in too. Virtually anyway. Buzz me when you get there. Signing off to get some sleep." His screen goes black.

I get to my feet too. "You'll buzz Jackson when you get *where*? What are you up to?" I'd be lying if I said seeing my brothers work as a team wasn't nice, but I have a bad feeling about whatever they're doing.

"They're not going anywhere until they take their dishes to the sink," Gran says. "No grandsons of mine will rush away from a meal and expect the women to clean up after them."

"Yes, Gran," all three of them mumble as they collect their plates.

Gran has always leaned a bit more toward the progressive side of things, but her feminism has ratcheted up a few notches since our grandad passed.

My brothers rinse their dishes at warp speed, place them in the dishwasher, then head to the door.

"For the last time, where are you going?" I ask.

"We're off to New York City to confront that Pork guy!" Ethan somehow says with a straight face.

"It's *Bacon*," I say. "And no, you are not! What are you gonna do? Wander around New York City and hope you bump into him?"

Sam, usually the stoic voice of reason, mumbles, "Seems like you're the one who was bumping into him. Over and over again."

"Gross, Sam! You need to never say that again. Also, you need to stop texting me every time I'm about to have sex!"

"What? I don't do that!" he insists.

"Every time your twin sense tells you I'm in danger…" I try to lead him to the realization without me having to say it again.

Sam gasps. "I'm actually sensing you're about to have sex?"

"Bingo," I say.

Gran smiles. "Twinship is truly a remarkable thing."

Ethan is getting impatient. "Gentlemen? Truck leaves in T-minus ten seconds!"

I throw my hands up. "Seriously, this is ridiculous. You don't even know where Bacon lives!"

"We do actually." Sam lifts his phone and shows me a screenshot of Bacon's apartment building.

"How did you—?"

Alex shakes his head at me and Sam. "You two should

really turn off sharing locations. You're twins, not boyfriend/girlfriend. Cut the cord, kids!"

Sam turns serious. "Cut the cord is a confusing idiom to use in this situation, Alex. Colleen and I are fraternal, so we didn't even share an amniotic sac in utero. Or a placenta. Cutting the cord implies we were somehow connected by an umbilical cord at one point, and that's simply not true."

Alex sighs. "It's just a saying!"

"Yeah," Sam says. "An inaccurate one."

"Sam," I say. "Back on track, please. This is a violation of a man's privacy."

He shrugs. "I was worried about you that day you missed the bus home. I tracked your location and saved the screenshot, figuring in the event of your murder, I could submit it as evidence in a court of law."

"Wow," Ethan mutters.

"That's what I'm saying," Alex whispers. "They gotta cut the cord."

"You know what, guys!?" I raise my voice. "I gotta cut the cord with all of you! Every single one of you! I mean, dammit! At what point are you going to respect me enough to let me deal with my own shit?"

"These children and their cussing." Gran shakes her head in disappointment.

"She curses a lot more than she used to, doesn't she?" Ethan says.

"Forgive me, Gran, but fuck yeah, I do, Ethan! You would too if you were me. You guys can't keep doing this."

"What? What do we do?" Alex asks.

"You sweep in whenever I have a problem and try to make it go away for me. You did it when those mean girls in middle school made fun of my training bra. You did it in high school when Bobby Hunter ditched me at prom. Ethan, you did it just last week at Tiddy's when that drunk guy called me 'babydoll.'

It's like you all think I can't handle my own life. Thankfully, you were wise enough to give your girlfriend space to handle her health, but you can't seem to give me the same respect."

Ethan starts, "Collie, we respect you! And we know you can handle yourself, but—"

"Did you ever think that maybe I'm happy about this baby?!" I yell.

The room goes silent.

Wow.

Did I really just say that?

I take a seat at the kitchen table, and for the first time since I got the news, I place my hands on my belly. It's hard to believe that just yesterday I attributed the slight roundness I'm feeling now to regular weight gain. It all feels so obvious now that I know what's really going on. I'm going to have a baby.

Gran approaches and places a soft, warm hand on my back. "Are you, sweetheart? You're happy?" She massages my shoulders like she used to after my parents died when I was carrying way too much sadness and stress for a kid so small.

I allow myself to lean into her.

"Having a baby is the last thing I planned or expected at this moment in my life... but, yeah." I look up at her and smile. "I think I'm happy."

"Then I am too, sweetheart." Gran leans forward and kisses the top of my head. "Whatever you need, we're here to support you."

"Or *not* support you as the case may be," Sam huffs, his feelings clearly hurt.

"Sam-Dan." I use my old nickname for him, so he knows we're cool. "I absolutely welcome my brothers' support. What I don't need is you guys running down to New York City to attack my..." I hesitate. "My, um—"

"I believe the term you are looking for is 'baby daddy,'" Ethan says.

"Yeah, I will *not* be calling him that." I laugh.

"To be clear," Alex says. "We had no intention of physically attacking him. The plan was just a good old-fashioned *verbal* assault."

"Good to know," I say. "But I have it from here."

"So?" Sam says. "What's your plan?"

"I'm going to see him myself."

CHAPTER 12
BACON

DAMN, IT'S COLD.

I wrap my coat around me tighter and turn onto my block, my mind spinning a mile a minute.

It's the day after my big win. I just met with the show producers about the next steps for my new restaurant. A fully-funded restaurant. I should be happy. The little kid I used to be could never have imagined an opportunity this massive landing in his lap. Everywhere that little kid looked he saw people working their tails off and only barely scraping by. When struggle is all you ever see, you don't let yourself dream of more.

But here I am now, the Season One winner of *Yes, Chef!* with more possibility in my pocket than I know what to do with.

So yeah, I should be happy.

But I can't stop thinking about her.

And that pisses me the hell off.

When I reach my building, the last person I expect to be shivering on my stoop is doing exactly that. The moment I see her, I'm transported back in time and flooded with memories. Her bright blue eyes sparkling at me in the studio audience when she held up her sign. Her gorgeous smile when she spotted my bookshelf. The way her breathy sighs skated across my skin when I was inside her.

This is not a woman to fantasize about.

This is the woman who lied to me and left me.

She rises to her feet when she sees me. "Congratulations on your win," she says after an awkward silence. She sounds sad and not at all like the dynamic woman I spent the night with all those months ago. "Can we talk?" she asks.

"That depends. Should I call you Cookie? Or Colleen? Or maybe you cycle through names depending on the day?" I try to keep my voice neutral, but the sarcasm is strong.

"Colleen is good." She winces. "I'm sorry about that. I'm sorry about everything. I'm sorry I lied to you. I'm sorry I ran off on you. Mostly, I'm sorry that I blew my chance with an incredible guy who made me feel like—"

"*Yes, Chef! Yes, Chef! Yes, Chef!*" a family shouts out the window of a passing cab. I give them a subtle wave. This has been happening more recently, with me getting recognized for the show. I can't say I'm comfortable with it, but overall, the interactions have been positive so far.

I clear my throat. "Sorry. You were saying?"

"So you're a celebrity now, huh?" She smiles.

"I wouldn't say that. Wait. That's not why you're here now, is it? Because suddenly I'm—"

"No," she says emphatically. "Of course not. No."

I want to believe her. But it is a bit suspect to disappear for months, then reappear the moment I get some level of notoriety.

An older couple walks by, holding hands. The man points and says to his wife, "Look, hon! It's your chef boy!" His wife gasps and approaches me. "You're even more adorable in person, sweetheart. We're so glad you won!"

"Oh, uh—Thank you, ma'am."

"Can I pinch your cheek? I'd love to pinch your cheek," she says earnestly.

"Why not?" I say with a shrug and jut my chin in her direction.

She startles me by pinching my ass instead. Then with a delighted squeal, she and her husband are gone.

"Not a celebrity, huh?" Colleen smirks.

"People are just being nice. It's the holiday season too, so there are lots of tourists in town. Actual New Yorkers don't give a shit. About anything."

"Gotcha," she says and stares at her feet.

"That wasn't a dig at you," I'm quick to explain. "You know, because you lied about being a New Yorker."

"Though technically, I *am* a New Yorker. Fork Lick *is* in New York," she says.

I narrow my eyes at her. "We both know that's not the same thing."

"You're right. We do." She stares at her feet some more.

She's nervous talking to me. And I hate it. What I hate even more is that I want to make things better for her. Easier.

"What would should we call your people?" I ask. "Fork Lickers? That sounds like an insult somehow."

"No, that's right. We are Fork Lickers. And generally, we're very proud to be Fork Lickers. Except for when we aren't." She pauses. "I'm not making much sense, am I?"

"Not really, no," I admit.

"Can we go somewhere and really talk?" she asks, just as a blustering cold wind whips past.

"Yeah, we can. Want to come inside?"

"I'd like that, thank you."

I guide her through the main door of my building, and we make our way through the lobby. A woman with gray hair and a tiny dog winks at me as she gets off the elevator, and we get on.

Colleen stifles a laugh as the double doors close.

I press the number for my floor. "It seems I resonate strongly with the older female population."

"I'm getting that. My grandmother is a big fan of yours as well. She calls you her 'sexy Bacon boy.'"

"Wow. I'm not sure how to respond to that."

"That's understandable. For what it's worth, she's a very cool lady. And she is single. I can make introductions sometime if you'd like," she jokes, and even though there's so much I need to understand about why things turned out the way they did, I'm so relieved that we're joking.

"I don't know about that. For the past few months, I've been pretty hung up on someone else."

She smiles shyly. Her cheeks, already pink from the cold outside, get even rosier.

We're quiet as the elevator ascends.

"So your grandmother watched the show, huh?"

She nods. "My whole family did actually."

"That must have been…interesting for you."

She smiles sadly. "Understatement of the century, sir."

The elevator doors open, and I quickly key into my apartment. She stands in the doorway, taking in the space.

Does she remember that night we shared here together?

I certainly do.

"Are you coming in?" I ask gently.

She snaps out of whatever trance she was in and says, "Yeah, yeah. Thanks."

"Can I take your coat?"

She reaches to unzip but thinks better of it and clutches her coat tighter, arms crossed over her middle. "Actually, I'll leave it on for now if you don't mind."

That's odd.

"Heat's on," I say. "And it's the old steam heat these old Upper West Side buildings are known for. The temperatures can get fairly tropical this time of year. But, hey, whatever makes you comfortable."

She walks the perimeter of the apartment, scanning the

bookshelves and finally landing in the kitchen area. Her hand runs back and forth over the marble countertop.

"We packed a lot of memories into one day, didn't we?" I say softly.

"We sure did." I could be mistaken, but her throat bobs, and I swear her eyes are glassier than they were a moment ago. "Could I possibly have a drink?"

"Of course. I can make some coffee?"

"I recently switched to decaf."

"Now I know you're not a New Yorker," I tease. "No self-respecting New Yorker says 'I recently switched to decaf.'"

She doesn't say anything, just laughs politely. That's what has me thrown right now. We're both being so... polite. That first day we met, there wasn't a polite bone in either of our bodies.

"Well, it's officially afternoon, so I could open a bottle of wine? Pour another mimosa, maybe?"

"Could I just have a glass of water?" she says.

It hits me what I just said. "'Another mimosa' wasn't a euphemism for—I mean, I know the last time we had mimosas we—I just—I'm not expecting—"

"I know you're not, Bacon."

"Okay, good," I sigh. "Water coming right up." I turn toward the kitchen, then turn immediately back to her.

"Can I say—" We both start at the same time.

"You, go," I laugh.

"No, you. Please." She slides onto a stool as I pour the glass of water and place it in front of her.

I take a deep breath and dive in. "Alright. You're an adult. I'm an adult. People have one-night stands all the time, and it's perfectly fine. I just—I mean, maybe I was mistaken, but that didn't feel like what we were doing. At all. I felt like we really connected."

"I did too," she says after a small sip.

She still seems so nervous.

"So? What went wrong?" I ask. "And why all the lies?"

She opens her mouth to speak.

"Before you answer that, let me make something really clear: Cookie or Colleen, New York or Fork Lick, publishing or teaching... it's all great. Obviously. What stumped me is why lie at all? It all seemed so arbitrary. I mean, you're not married, right?"

"Right. No. I mean, yes, I'm not married." She rubs the crease between her eyebrows.

"Is lying about random things how you get your kicks, then?"

"No, not at all—"

"Then what? Because—"

"Dude, if you'd let me speak, I'll explain everything to you!"

Her sass is back. A glimmer of that wild woman I met four months ago is showing her face again.

"My apologies." I pull up the other stool and sit beside her. "I'm a talker."

"It's okay. I like that you're a talker. So many guys are 'the strong, silent types.' Between my father, grandfather, and four brothers, I've had enough of the strong silent types to last me a lifetime, believe me."

"Four brothers!" I say. "Wow! Any sisters?"

"Nope, I am the lone Bedd sister," she says, and I'd have to be completely dense not to pick up on the layers of frustration lurking under that statement. But I don't press for more information. It's this talker's turn to really listen.

"You know what? That's actually a good place for me to start," she says more to herself than to me. She takes a deep breath. "I was in a weird headspace when I met you that day. Life at home has been pretty topsy-turvy lately. And not because I am in a rocky relationship or anything like that. Relationships—of the romantic variety anyway—haven't really ever been my thing. I've *wanted* them to be, but—ugh!"

She chides herself. "You don't need my whole emotional history."

"I'm here. I'm listening. Why don't you just take it slow?"

"I actually think it would help if I got it all out really fast. Like ripping off a bandage. Would that be okay?"

"Sure, whatever you—"

She cuts me off and talks at warp speed. "My parents died when I was ten. Car crash. Hit by a runaway semi on their way home from celebrating their anniversary. They went on this romantic sightseeing trip—they were always doing *something* romantic—and we stayed with my grandparents while they were gone. We had no idea of course that they would *stay* gone and our grandparents would essentially become our parents from that moment forward. Needless to say, their death messed me up. My brothers too, but god forbid we ever *talk* about it, you know? Oh yeah, those four brothers I mentioned? They're all incredibly sexy. I know, I know, that sounds bizarre hearing a woman admit that her brothers are sexy, but I have eyes, and lord knows I have *ears*—my whole town never shuts up about how attractive they are. 'The Bedd brothers, the Bedd brothers!' It's all I hear. I swear I am just a vehicle for people to get to my hot-ass farmer brothers. Oh, right, I live on a farm. Did I mention that yet?"

"No, uh. Not yet, no," I say. Wow, she's a whirlwind right now.

"And guess what? We might *lose* that farm! Hahaha!" She laughs, though it's not a particularly happy sound. "What a cliché, right? My grandad died this year and we found out he owed an insane amount of money. Thanks for the heads-up, Gramps! I've been living with my grandmother again, helping her grieve and trying like hell to dig the farm out of debt all while continuing to work as a kindergarten teacher basically for pennies and having no personal life whatsoever."

Maybe you should take a breath?" I suggest. "It sounds like you've been dealing with a lot."

"Don't worry, I'm getting to my point. The morning I came into the city for your show, I'd hit my breaking point. I told myself I deserved one day to be wild. To not be me. When I saw you on the soundstage, something just... clicked. I don't know how to explain it. Colleen would never scribble a provocative sign to a stranger, but *Cookie* would. I went for it, and I'm so sorry to say I didn't concern myself with your feelings. That is, until we were full make-out city in that Town Car, and you said, 'There's nothing I hate more in this world than liars.'" She finally slows down and breathes deep. "When I promised I wouldn't lie to you, I meant it. I kept my promise from that moment forward."

"That night, when you said—and I quote—'Your pork sword should be named the eighth wonder of the world...'"

"Totally meant it."

"And when you said my 'stomach is the real Stairway to Heaven' then proceeded to blow me while performing air guitar on my abs?"

"What can I say, you made me feel musical."

We have a good laugh at that.

She looks deep into my eyes. "Please know, I snuck out the next morning because I was embarrassed and ashamed, not because I didn't want to see you again. I've basically thought of nothing and no one else since. And none of what I just said is me making excuses for my behavior that day, but—"

"Colleen?

"Yeah?" Her eyes are wide and hopeful.

"I fucking loved your behavior that day. Your behavior that day was superb."

"Back atcha, stud!"

She laughs and lays her head on my shoulder. It's the first time she's touched me since I found her waiting on my front stoop. Touching her again, however simple the touch may be, feels like coming home.

"You know," I whisper. "I never did get to take you on a real New York City date."

"You're right, you didn't," she sasses.

"In my defense, Cookie told me you didn't want to date; you only wanted to fuck."

"I think we've already agreed that while Cookie was fun, she suffered from having a one-track mind. However, *Colleen* is interested in all aspects of the human experience. Colleen would be honored to go on a real New York City date with you."

"How does right now sound?" I ask.

"You want to take Colleen on a date right now?" She laughs.

"I mean, if she's not busy?" I tease.

She sighs, and the air in the room gets serious again.

"Am I missing something?" I ask tentatively.

Colleen places a hand on my forearm. "Bacon, I would love nothing more than for you to take me on a date right now."

"But...?"

"But there's one more thing you need to know first."

I brace myself for the worst.

But instead, she says...

"I'm pregnant. With your baby."

CHAPTER 13
COLLEEN

"THAT'S THE BEST NEWS I'VE EVER HEARD IN MY GODDAMN LIFE."

What did he just say?

He must have heard me wrong. Or I heard him wrong. Either way, right now something is very wrong.

"Um. I think you might be confused, Bacon. I just said you're going to be a father. Well, the word father is probably presumptuous, being that we barely know each other, and I just got finished groveling at your feet for lying to you, but—"

"Are you lying about this?"

"Absolutely not."

"Then let's get past all that and move forward. You're serious? You're pregnant?"

"Very much pregnant, yes."

"And you know it's—"

"A hundred percent yours, yes."

He positively beams at me. Of all the reactions I thought he might give me—anger, frustration, detachment, worry, resentment—I did not anticipate his sheer joy.

"You're happy about this," I marvel.

"Fucking ecstatic, yes. I've always wanted to be a dad."

"Wow..." I pause while I process that. "Do you, uh—

Would you like to see?" I nod toward my belly, still cloaked by my heavy winter coat. It strikes me that the last time I sat in this kitchen, I was completely naked, and now, here I am, all nervous and covered from head to toe.

"Please," he says. "If you're comfortable."

"Sure. Of course." I stand and slowly unbutton my coat while he watches my every move. It feels like a bizarre fully clothed strip tease. And it is ten times more vulnerable and nerve-wracking than if I was actually showing my bare skin.

Getting physically naked is easy. Emotional nudity is a whole other ball game.

I'm left standing in my plaid winter dress and thick tights, my small baby bump protruding just enough to be obvious if you're on the lookout for it. I fan myself with my hand. "Whew, I was getting hot in that thing. You weren't kidding about the steam heat in these apartments."

Bacon gets to his feet, his face soft and his eyes trained on my midsection. "So why did you just sit there then, all swaddled and suffering?"

"Well, I felt like I should keep my belly under wraps until I officially gave you the news. Plus, I felt a little shy about my second first impression with you being one where you think 'wow, she's been packing on the pounds!'"

"I would never think that. Look at you," he says on a reverent sigh. "I didn't think it was possible for you to be any more gorgeous. But here we are. Here *you* are."

This guy. He is something else.

He lowers to his knees right in front of me and reaches his hands out. "May I?"

"May you...? Oh, touch my—? Sure, go right ahead. Touch, touch."

Is it wrong that the second his big, strong hands land on my belly, my arousal goes through the roof? I hadn't realized until this moment that the feeling was steadily building since I first saw him turn the corner and walk up to me sitting outside his apartment. I'm starting to think as long as Bacon is around, my internal temperature will be set to hot.

"You're very sweet, Bacon, but listen, I have no expectations here. You can be as involved or uninvolved as you want."

"Involved," he says emphatically. "I want to be involved."

"Really?" I ask, voice breathy.

He rises to stand and cups my cheeks in both hands. "Unequivocally."

"Well, okay then," I whisper.

He leans in and kisses me.

And for the first time since I ran out of his apartment that summer morning, my shoulders relax, the tension in my forehead eases, and dare I say, I feel hopeful and happy.

"I have good news and bad news," Bacon says softly when he releases my lips. "Which one do you want first?"

"Bad news. You should always choose the bad news first."

He wraps his arms around my lower back and pulls me closer until my slightly round belly nestles against his flat one. "Our official New York City date will have to wait."

"And the good news?" I circle my arms loosely around his neck.

"I get to visit Fork Lick after all."

That tension that slid off my shoulders and fled my forehead a moment ago? It immediately creeps back in with those words.

"Why, uh, why, uh, why would you visit Fork Lick?" I ask.

"Are you stuttering?" He laughs.

"I think I am, yeah."

He strokes my hair and tucks a loose piece behind my ear. "The grandmother and four brothers you mentioned… I imagine they have feelings about some random man getting their granddaughter/sister pregnant?"

"They do, but—"

"Well, I think the only gentlemanly thing for me to do is to pay them a visit as soon as possible. Last I checked, buses run every hour at half past the hour. If I pack my bag quickly, we can be there before dinner."

He pauses and flashes me that beautiful smile.

"Colleen Bedd? It's time for you to bring home the Bacon."

CHAPTER 14
BACON

I DON'T GET OUT OF THE CITY ENOUGH.

That's what I'm thinking as I sit on this bus heading north toward Greene County, a sleeping Colleen resting against my shoulder.

Even in the wintertime, this scenery is stunning. The snow-covered hills and the tree branches encased in ice give off this vibe of tranquility that calls to me. I can only imagine how beautiful this area is in the fall when the leaves start changing.

I'm trying to remember the last time I really immersed myself in nature. While I was shooting *Yes, Chef!*, I took the occasional walk in Central Park when I could, but I'm not sure that counts when you can look up in any direction and still see skyscrapers all around. And before that, I was in Philly, working in the kitchen in any restaurant that would have me.

It's strange the stories we tell about ourselves. For as long as I can remember, I've heard myself insisting, "I'm a city guy." But I'm starting to wonder if that was ever even true. Because the moment I get a taste of fresh air and a big sky—*space*—I feel contentment and possibility like I never have before.

My phone sounds with a text and stirs Colleen awake.

Damn, I should have put the thing on silent.

A glance confirms what I already suspect. For the past decade, he reaches out periodically, requesting to see me and asking me if I can forgive him at some point. Letters, emails, texts... you name it. For the most part, I don't respond. Since seeing me on TV, though, the frequency of his messages has increased. Must be hard when people congratulate you on your son's big win and you have no relationship with that son whatsoever.

Well, that's not my problem, Dad.

Colleen yawns. "How long have I been asleep?"

"You passed out as soon as we hit the Palisades Parkway."

"Huh. I didn't realize I was so tired. Sorry I left you without my stellar conversation skills," she jokes.

"Oh, that's alright. I got to experience your stellar snoring and drooling skills."

"I do not drool!" she protests, then looks sheepish when I point at the damp spot on my shirtsleeve. "Sorry."

"Lady, you can drool on me any day."

She registers the scenery flying past our window. "Ahhh. We're set to arrive in Climax in approximately... fifteen minutes."

"We plan to climax while we're on this bus?" I whisper, then peer over the seats at our fellow passengers.

"No!" She swats my arm. "The closest sizeable town near Fork Lick is called Climax. That's where our bus is stopping. FYI, my twin brother's girlfriend, Diane, will pick us up from the station."

"Sounds good." I laugh, then give her a little nudge. "Nervous?"

"Beyond nervous, yeah. You?"

"Meeting your four disapproving brothers? You bet I'm nervous."

"If it helps, you'll only meet three disapproving brothers

today. My younger brother Jackson is a musician, and he's in LA."

"That's very cool."

"Yeah, it is. We're super proud of him."

I gesture to my bag. "I'm suddenly realizing I might not have packed appropriate clothing for a farm. Will you have me milking cows and chasing chickens? I can always hit the mall if I need something good for rolling around in dung."

"Rolling around in dung?" She laughs.

"I'm a city guy. What do I know?"

"We don't even have a mall," Colleen says. "But you should be fine with what you brought. It's the offseason, and we're mostly a soybean farm anyway. If you have your heart set on rolling in dung, though, we can always visit Alex's creamery and find you a cowpie or two."

"I appreciate you being so accommodating," I joke.

"You're very welcome," she says with a smirk, then turns more serious. "And I appreciate you making this trip with me. I know I was skittish when you first suggested it. But I agree. It's the right thing to do."

"You mentioned the farm is in trouble. How much debt are we talking about?

"Uhhhhh," she hesitates.

"I don't mean to pry. I know money can be a sensitive subject to talk about, but I was thinking… maybe I can help."

"You would do that?"

"Colleen, you're carrying my baby." He pauses. "That sounded a little patriarchal, didn't it?"

She laughs. "Maybe a little bit."

"*Our* baby sounds better, right?"

"It does."

"Okay. You're carrying our baby. *Of course* I will help your family however I can. Are you comfortable talking about how much debt the place is in?"

"I guess so?" She sighs. "When my grandad died and we

first got the bad news, we were looking at around three-quarters of a million."

"Ouch," I say. "Not pretty."

"Yeah, it was downright ugly. But we've made some incredible progress over the past year. We used to be exclusively a soybean farm, but we've diversified our offerings a bit. Strawberries are a big thing for us now. We actually have a surplus in the freezer that we're looking to utilize somehow. We've spiffed up the farm stand on my brother Alex's dairy farm down the road, and that's been a new support for Bedd Fellows." She scans my face. "We've made other improvements and started other initiatives too, but I don't want to bore you."

"Colleen, you could never bore me."

"Long story short, we're getting there. But wintertime is hard for farmers, and there's still quite a way to go before we're out of the woods. I just want to make things better for my gran. She's been through so much. I mean, can you imagine losing your only son and then having to raise his five children? And then after all that, right when you're supposed to be entering your golden years, your husband dies and leaves you deep in a surprise mountain of debt?"

"Yeah, that's incredibly rough. Your grandfather doesn't sound like a great guy."

"Excuse me?" Colleen's expression turns hard.

Shit. I've overstepped.

I put my hands up in a defense position. "That came out harsher than I intended. What I meant to say was—it's a father's job to provide and—"

"My grandfather was a *great* guy, Bacon. And he provided his ass off! Can you imagine suddenly having five extra mouths to feed? And, as you'll see in approximately fifteen minutes, my brothers and I aren't exactly easy! We're a handful! He also made sure we had what we needed. He sent us to college and—"

"Colleen?" She takes a breath and gives me her full attention. "I misspoke. That was insensitive of me, and I'm sorry."

"Well, okay then." She stares out the passing scenery in silence for a few breaths, then chuckles. "I'm the first one to talk crap about my family. But they're *my* family, you know? Guess I'm more protective of them than I realized."

"You're lucky to have each other," I say softly.

"Yeah. We really are. How about you?" she asks. "You haven't said much about your family."

I shrug. "Not much to tell."

"Come on, Chef, give me something. I don't know a single human who doesn't have family drama to spill."

"You called me Chef." I smile.

She smiles back and places a hand on my thigh. "Brings back memories, doesn't it?"

"It sure does."

I place my hand over hers. She flips her palm and weaves her fingers with mine. Then she gives my hand a squeeze, encouraging me to talk.

How do I explain this?

I pull out my phone and pull up my messaging app. "What do you see here?"

"Looks like a long thread of unanswered texts." She squints at my screen. "Who is… MWSM?"

"Man Who Sired Me," I say.

Colleen's eyes go wide. "Wow. That's really what you call your father?"

"I don't call him anything. I don't speak to him." I slip my phone back into my pocket. As much as he deserves my silence, I don't feel proud when I see how many times he's reached out over the years and how many times I've ignored him. "You must think that's terrible, huh? You lost your dad. And here I am with a very much alive father who I refuse to speak to."

"I don't think you're terrible. I think families can be... complicated."

"How's this for complicated? When I was eight years old, my mom discovered my dad had been living a double life. It sounds like a soap opera episode when I phrase it like that, but that's what it was. A double life. He had my mom and me in Philly. And a whole other family in Pittsburgh."

"Oh my god," she says and squeezes my hand tighter.

"Yeah. Double of everything for him while his wife and kid were barely scraping by. Can't exactly pay the bills with a truckload of lies."

I watch the proverbial light bulb go off in Colleen's head. "That's why you were so upset when I lied to you."

"Yes," I say and lean into her warmth. "But we're past that now."

"I hope so," she says, but the doubt in her tone is clear.

"Colleen?" I place a kiss on her forehead. "We are."

She snuggles up closer to me.

I wrap an arm around her and continue. "My mom kicked him out after she put the pieces together. She did her best with me, but her downward spiral started and just never stopped. As a kid, I thought she was just sad, but now, as an adult, I can see she was clinically depressed. When I was around twelve and it became clear my mom couldn't take good care of me, my buddy Trent's family took me in. Raised me as their own. My mom passed the summer I turned eighteen."

"God, Bacon. I'm so sorry you went through all that."

I try to make light of the situation. "I'm sorry that you have a baby daddy with daddy issues!"

She chuckles good-naturedly beside me, but I can sense her unease with everything I just told her.

"Hey." I tilt her chin up to look at me. "I wanted to give you the whole story because—as you well know by now—honesty is important to me. But you have nothing to worry about." I pause. "I saw this news story once. It was about these two brothers. They grew up in the same home. Same dad. This dad was bad news. Constantly in trouble with the law. You name a crime, this guy committed it at some point. Fast-forward a few decades and one brother grew up to be just like him—always struggling, always going down the wrong path. The other brother stayed away from drugs, studied hard, and got a good job. Eventually, that brother started a family and took excellent care of his wife and kids. This news segment interviewed the brothers separately and asked them the same question: 'How do you explain the way your life has turned out?' And the wildest thing happened. They answered the question in the same way: 'How else could my life have turned out with the father I had?'"

"Hmm," she says softly.

I could be imagining it, but I swear her expression goes cloudy at that.

"I need you to know I'm the second guy, Colleen. I'm going to be a great father not in spite of the bad example I was given but *because* of it."

"Oh my god, we're here," she says, her spine going ramrod straight.

The bus pulls into a dirt parking lot beside a small gas station. Piles of snow surround the lot, and about a dozen cars idle, presumably waiting to pick up friends and family members like us visiting from the city.

We descend the steep steps and are immediately greeted by a young woman in red-and-white-striped pajamas and a fluffy green robe. It's five in the afternoon, so either she's very late getting her day started or she's an early-to-bed kind of gal.

"Diane, what the hell are you wearing?" Colleen asks.

"Holiday jammies," the woman says matter-of-factly. "Is this not something your family usually does?"

"Never, no." Colleen shakes her head.

"Interesting." Diane cocks her head to the side, then snaps back to the moment. "Hi! You must be—"

"Yes, yes," Colleen jumps into action. "Let me introduce you. Diane, this is my—This is Bacon. Bacon, this is Diane. Did I mention that Diane is dating my twin brother, Sam?"

"You did." I smile and offer my hand to Diane. "Hi. It's a pleasure to meet you. Thank you for the ride."

She gives my hand a firm shake. "Nice to meet you too! And no problem at all! I think Colleen figured I was the most neutral party possible to greet you." She bows slightly. "Consider me Switzerland."

"Am I about to walk into a war zone?" I ask with a nervous laugh.

"Everything will be fine," Diane says with a tight smile and pats me on the back.

Oh boy.

Here goes nothing.

CHAPTER 15
COLLEEN

WHEN WE PULL UP TO BEDD FELLOWS FARM, MY BROTHERS' trucks are all parked in a row. Every window in the house is lit. Sam stands in the doorway, then immediately disappears from view when we approach.

I pull Diane to the side as Bacon removes our bags from the trunk.

"What is this, an ambush?"

"Consider it a welcome," Diane says diplomatically.

"They could at least wait for us to get settled before they descend."

"Don't worry. Gran gave quite a speech this afternoon. They will all be on their best behavior, and they know their only job is to offer you and your baby daddy encouragement and support."

Bacon joins us with the bags.

"Brace yourself, buddy," I say.

"You're not a vegetarian, are you?" Diane asks.

"No," he says. "Why?"

"They may have gone a little overboard with—Well. You'll see."

The moment we open the door, we are swarmed by a sea of Bedds in red and white stripes. There is a chorus of "You're here!" and "Welcome to Bedd Fellows Farm, Bacon!" and an unfortunate "Way to knock up my sister, sir!"

"First of all, what are you all wearing?" I wince and block my eyes with my forearm. The stripes are blinding me.

"Gran thought it would be nice if we wore matching holiday jammies this year," Alex says with practiced and painful enthusiasm. He and Ethan are bulging out of their too-small pajamas, looking like giant, uncomfortable barber poles.

"She did?" I whip my head left and right, looking for the Gran in question.

She emerges from the crowd, wearing her own striped cotton pajamas and carrying two additional folded sets in her hands. "With my first great-grandbaby on the way, I thought it was the perfect time to start some new traditions."

"Wow. That's… Okay, cool," I stammer.

"These are for you." She hands a small pair to me. "And these…" She hands an extra-large set to Bacon.

"Thank you, ma'am." Bacon smiles warmly at my grandmother as he takes the pajamas. "And thank you for welcoming me into our home."

"And into our sister's vagina," my twin murmurs.

"Sam-Dan! Geezuz!" I scold, right as Diane gives him that "cut it out" gesture people do across their throats. "Were you also the one who said 'Way to knock up our sister, sir' when we walked in just now?"

"You know I don't always get social cues right!" Samuel says. "I'm trying over here, Sis." He turns to the man next to me, who is stifling a laugh. "My apologies, Bacon."

"Not a problem, Sam. I'm thrilled to meet you."

They shake hands, which quickly turns into an awkward backslapping bro-hug of sorts I've never seen my brother do.

Diane leans over and whispers, "He's trying new things."

"I can see that," I murmur, then raise my voice. "Everyone? This is Bacon."

"Hi, Bacon!" they answer with a cheery choreographed wave.

"Hi… everyone," he answers and gives a small wave of his own.

"Okay, you guys have to stop with the creepy unison stuff. Let's just get it all on the table so we can shake off the awkwardness and have a nice night, shall we? Bacon? This is my family. You met Gran. Ethan goes with Lia, Alex goes with Molly, Sam goes with Diane—"

"Like on *Cheers*?" Bacon says cheerfully.

"Yes, like on *Cheers*," I answer quickly and keep powering through. "There's also Jackson, who—as far as I know—is single." I turn to my brothers. "Should we be expecting a video call from Jackson for this family meeting as well?"

"No," Ethan says. "He couldn't make this one."

"Darn!" I say sarcastically. "I guess one of you will have to fill him in on whatever happens tonight, then."

"I'm already assigned to that task," Samuel says.

"Fantastic. Wouldn't want anyone to be uninformed. And this…" I use presentational arms like I'm a beautiful model on a game show, making sure the contestants all see the prize they're competing to win. "…is Bacon. His birthname is Harold Hotman, but we don't use that name because it reminds him of his deadbeat dad, Harold Hotman Senior."

"Oh dear," Gran says and covers her mouth.

"I'm sorry," I whisper to Bacon. "Was that too harsh? I'm trying to get us through this as painlessly as possible."

"Harsh, maybe," he says. "But not untrue. Hello, everyone. I know these circumstances are a bit… nontraditional. And I can only assume that you are wondering what my intentions are toward your sister." He looks at Gran. "And in your case, ma'am, your granddaughter."

My brothers confirm his assumption to be true with their crossed arms and silence.

"Well, I can assure you all that I want nothing but the very best for Colleen. I'll be the first to admit that we don't know each other incredibly well yet. But I couldn't be more excited to learn everything I possibly can about her." He turns his attention directly to me now and softens his voice. "I don't want you to feel an ounce of pressure, Colleen. But I need you to know I'm thrilled about this baby. I'm thrilled to be having a baby with *you*. And I'm here for you every step of the way. Whatever you need."

"That's, um. That's really, really nice," I say with tears in my eyes.

He leans down and kisses me.

I kiss him back.

In front of my whole family.

When we break from the kiss, it registers that the whole room is whooping and clapping. Even my twin looks happy.

Sam shouts, "Alright, everybody! Let's celebrate the happy couple with some pork products!"

With that, my brothers gather around Bacon and pull him into the dining area.

I stay a few feet behind and lean closer to Molly.

"Pork products?" I ask.

Molly responds, "They wanted to be welcoming of Bacon's culture, so they really went all in on pig products."

"Oh, dear god," I say as we reach the table and see the spread of glistening meats.

Bacon winks at me from across the table. He apparently loves this.

"Behold," Sam says, gesturing toward the table covered in food.

"Behold!" Alex repeats in a British accent and raises one pinky like he's holding a cup and saucer brimming with tea.

This is a silly thing we Bedd siblings have always done when one of us says a "fancy" word.

Ethan and I follow suit. We shout "Behold!" in our own

attempts at a British accent and each lift a pinky finger as well.

All four of us mime drinking from our imaginary teacups.

Gran smiles and shakes her head. "You kids."

Sam continues, "For our menu tonight, we have bacon-wrapped dates, bacon-wrapped scallops, bacon-wrapped asparagus..."

"So much bacon-wrapping," I say under my breath to Lia.

Ethan chimes in, "We also have bacon, lettuce, and tomato sandwiches—more commonly known as BLTs. And for some variety—the pig is nothing if not a versatile animal—we have sliced pork, pork sausages, and a candied ham."

My brothers look so proud.

Gran's hands are clasped over her heart, her eyes shining.

"Thank you, everyone, for this weird and wonderful welcome," Bacon says with an obvious lump in his throat. "I'm truly touched by your thoughtfulness. I think we'd be wise to have some antacids on hand for tomorrow morning, but other than that, I don't think there's anything else to say other than... Let's eat!"

Sam responds with a raucous, "You heard the man! Let's eat!"

CHAPTER 16
BACON

How in the world did I end up here?

Yesterday, I was fighting off the cold of New York City, feeling more alone than ever. Today, I'm sitting in a bar in Fork Lick, NY, with three burly farmers, and we're all wearing matching striped holiday pajamas.

"Tiddy's Bar, huh?" I say to the guys after a sip of beer. "Isn't this a family-friendly town? You'd think they'd come up with a more appropriate name than that."

"The owner's last name is Tiddy. It's his bar. What can ya do?" Alex shrugs and cracks open another brew.

A few minutes pass in easy silence.

"It's bold of you guys to head out in public wearing these jammies. Really speaks to your confidence in your masculinity."

"It's really just about never disappointing our grandmother," Ethan says. "When I suggested we change into our civilian clothes before heading out, she looked like Baabara had just died—"

"Lord help us when that day finally comes," Alex grumbles.

"Will never happen," Sam says. "Baabara is immortal."

"I've got to meet this sheep!" I say jovially.

"Oh, you will," Ethan says ominously. "Anyway. Gran wants us to keep the jammies on? We keep the jammies on. It's the least we can do." He takes another swig of beer. "Thanks for going along with it, Bacon."

"My pleasure. It's nice getting an up-close look at the inner workings of a big, happy American family."

"Ehhhh," all three guys say at once.

"Sorry, I don't speak Bedd man grunt," I joke.

"I'll take this one," Alex says. "'Ehhhh' means we're big and we're American but can't say we've always necessarily been *happy*."

I nod. "Understood. It's gotta be a rough road when you lose your parents so young."

"That it is," Ethan says. "Sounds like you know a little something about that too, though."

"I do. My story's different. But yeah, I do."

"The way I see it, all we can do as a generation is try to do a better job than the one before us," Ethan says.

"Hear, hear!" I clink my beer bottle with his, and we drink.

Alex shifts uncomfortably on his barstool. "What the hell, man? Mom and Dad did a great job. It's not their fault they fucking *died*."

"Simmer down, dude. I'm not saying anything against Mom and Dad. They did do a good job." Ethan pauses. "For what they knew at the time."

"What the hell does that mean?" Alex is getting heated now.

"It means... don't you ever wish our family talked more when we were growing up?"

Alex huffs. "Our house was nonstop talking. Constant noise."

"No, I think I know what Ethan means," Sam chimes in. "Dad was never the type to talk about his feelings. Or concern himself with ours. Mom either, really. I mean, I never doubted they loved us, but they didn't exactly express stuff like that."

"Except to each other," Alex says.

"Except to each other," Ethan agrees.

Sam places his empty beer bottle on the table. "You know I'm a little embarrassed to admit this, but I don't think I had any semblance of emotional intelligence until Diane came into my life."

"Same for me with Lia," Ethan says.

Alex mutters. "Me too with Molly."

They turn to me expectantly. Seems like it's my turn to say that I too had a hard time expressing myself before the woman in my life came along. I want to fit in with these guys and be part of the conversation, but that just wasn't the case for me.

I clear my throat. "I, uh—I learned at a pretty early age that talking about your feelings is vital if you want to live any kind of quality life. And listen, that's not a humble brag by any means. I just think after seeing my mom suffer so much with her own mental health, I knew I had to stay on top of mine. She didn't feel like she had anyone to talk to, which destroyed her. It's possible I've gone a bit extreme in the other direction." I let out a soft chuckle. "Colleen says I'm quite the 'talker,'"

"She says that because the poor girl grew up with four punks like us, who didn't know a healthy emotion from a hole in the ground." Ethan laughs.

"I don't know." I smile. "You guys seem alright to me."

"You're alright too, Bacon," Sam says. "I'm glad she has you."

"Did I just get the twin brother approval?" I joke.

"You did," he says. "Take good care of her and that baby, okay?"

"It will be the great honor of my life," I say seriously, then proceed to shake the hand of each of Colleen's brothers.

Alex's eyebrows are raised as he looks around the table. "Is this what Tiddy's nights will be now that Bacon's part of the family? Full of male bonding, shared trauma, and healthy emotional discourse? I've made my peace with going to therapy, but geez."

"I promise I'll keep a lid on it when I can." I laugh.

"All good," Alex says with the hint of a smile. "Let 'er rip, man."

The guys move on to other, more lighthearted topics, but I can't shake the warm feeling blooming in my chest.

I'm part of the family.

———

We're several hours into our time at Tiddy's, and one thing is clear: The Bedd Boys are drunk.

Who am I kidding? We're *all* drunk.

"Hey, guys," I slur slightly. "Do you think Colleen was mad that I came out with you guys tonight instead of staying home with her? Because she seemed a little mad."

"Why would she be mad?" Ethan waves a dismissive hand.

"Oh, she was mad alright," Sam says definitively.

"Shit. Really?" I whine.

"For sure," Sam says. "But she's mostly mad at herself for *being* mad."

"How do you know this?" I ask. "Did she text you?"

"Nope. Twin-sense." Sam points two fingers to his forehead, then shoots them out into the air a few times like they're picking up a signal of sorts.

Alex throws up his hands. "Here we go with the twin-sense thing again."

"Dude, it's real!" Sam says.

"I don't doubt that it's real. But that doesn't mean we want to hear about it all the damn time! You and Colleen have a connection we singleton siblings could never understand. We get it!"

"Don't listen to him," Sam says to me. "He's just jealous he was all alone in utero, and I had a built-in friend."

Alex glares at his brother. "Yeah, that's totally it."

Sam ignores him and focuses on me. "She wants you to bond with us. But she's also afraid for that to happen. She has this thing in her head that everyone uses her to get to us, which is—"

"Ridiculous," Ethan finishes Sam's sentence for him.

"Maybe not so ridiculous," Alex offers. "How about Ginny Quick?"

Sam groans.

"And April Simmons?"

Ethan groans.

"And any number of girls who were gunning for me in high school," Alex continues.

Sam quips, "Wow, your confidence certainly surges six beers in."

"I'm just saying, Colleen has justification for her fear."

"No offense, guys, but I'm way more interested in your sister than I am in you." I laugh.

"A quick text to reassure her probably wouldn't hurt." Sam shrugs.

"You're right, Sam. I will quick-text her!" An idea forms in my drunken brain as I grab my phone. I start typing, then hesitate. "I hate that I don't know this, but what is Colleen's middle name?"

"Murphy," Ethan says.

"Her name is Colleen Murphy Bedd?" I marvel.

"It was our mom's maiden name," Alex says. "They didn't really think that decision through."

"Well, I think it's beautiful. Just like your sister." With that, I fire off a free-flowing text with little-to-no concern for how it will be perceived on the other end.

> Colleen. Colleen. Colleen Murphy Bedd.

> Thank you for that time in my apartment when you gave me head.

> Your brothers are fun, your brothers are neat;

> But you are a queen and I bow down at your feet.

> We're going to be scorching, just wait and see.

> All I need is you. You're the one for me.

> I know that our relationship is still brand spankin' new,

> But what can I do? I'm head over heels in love with you.

I hand my phone over to Sam. "I just sent that. What do you think?"

"That's, uh—That's… wow, I mean, that's really something."

"Thanks! Hey, guys. Can I overstep?"

"Overstep on…what exactly?" Ethan asks warily.

"Your family business," I say. "Your farm business, more specifically. Colleen told me about the struggles you've been having, and I want to help. How can I help?"

"You could hand over that massive check you just got from *Yes, Chef!*" Alex's face gives me no clues as to whether or not he's joking.

"Alex!" Sam scolds. "That is so many levels of obnoxious."

"It's actually not!" I assure them. "I'd hand that money over to you all right now if I could, but the contract conditions are clear: all prize money is to be used for the opening of my new restaurant and the opening of my new restaurant only. I don't even receive the money outright. There is a special account that tracks my team's spending, clocking where each payment goes."

"Whoa, you have a *team*?" Alex says.

"It's strange, but yeah, I do. Right now, they're researching potential locations for the place based on my suggestions. They should be emailing me some possibilities Monday morning."

"Where are you hoping to set up shop?" Ethan asks.

"Well, I was planning on the Philadelphia area where I grew up and lived until the show started, but now I'm not so sure."

"You should start a restaurant in Fork Lick," Alex suggests.

"Alex, come on," Sam says. "The producers of his show want this place to be successful. A small town like Fork Lick is not the place for that."

"Are you kidding me?" Alex's voice rises. "You think the people of Fork Lick won't support a brand-new restaurant helmed by a sexy reality TV star?"

"You think I'm sexy, huh?" I run my hands down my abs and make googly eyes at Alex. He just stares back at my inebriated self.

"Too much?" I say sheepishly.

"Too much," he confirms, then quickly continues. "What kind of food are we talking about here?"

"Comfort food," I say, getting serious again. "Fried chicken, meatloaf, shepherd's pie, corn chowder… that sort of thing. But all with my own Bacon twist."

"That's fucking perfect!" Alex says. "Fork Lickers will support the shit out of that, and I guarantee you people from Climax will travel in for it, and folks from the city will too."

"I'm in!" I say.

"Wait. You're in?" Ethan says in disbelief.

"Well, I can't exactly raise a baby with your sister from a city nearly four hours away. I'm tired of making decisions

based on who I used to be instead of who I am now. I auditioned for *Yes, Chef!* on a whim. It was a shot in the dark, just
to try something different and shake things up. And look at
all the good that one decision has already brought into my
life! I wanna do it. I want to start my restaurant in Fork Lick."

"Alright!" the guys cheer.

"Now, I just need the right building and location."

Sam slams a hand on the table. "I know just the place."

CHAPTER 17
COLLEEN

I'M LYING IN THE SAME TWIN BED I'VE SLEPT IN SINCE I WAS A little girl, staring at the same ceiling where I placed hundreds of tiny glow-in-the-dark stars all those years ago, when a text from Bacon comes through.

He's in love with me?

He can't possibly be in love with me.

This is all moving too fast.

And I'm freaking out.

I do what I've always done when I'm anxious and can't sleep at night. I head downstairs to raid the family fridge.

I trudge downstairs as quietly as I can, trying not to wake my grandmother. That woman is the lightest sleeper there ever was. When we were teenagers, there was never any hope of sneaking in past curfew. One step through the creaky front door and she'd be padding down the hall in her bathrobe and slippers a moment later telling us "rules are rules for a reason."

I flick the light switch in the kitchen and nearly jump out of my skin when I find Gran sitting at the kitchen table with a mug of tea.

"Boo," she says with an impish grin.

"What the hell, Gran?" I place a hand over my rapidly beating heart.

"What? I can't enjoy a cup of tea in my own kitchen?"

"Sure, you can, but in the pitch black? What were you doing?"

She ignores my question and raps on the table twice, startling me.

"I'm glad you're here. It's time we had 'The Talk.'"

You've got to be kidding me.

"Please don't tell me you mean the sex talk," I say as I grab a bunch of grapes from the refrigerator and put them in a bowl.

"What other talk is there?"

"Gran," I say as I take a seat beside her. "I'm rapidly approaching thirty. If you wanted to have the sex talk, we probably should have had it—oh, I don't know—nearly two decades ago?" I lean back in my chair and smooth my pajamas over my baby bump. "As you can see, I figured it out."

"Clearly, you figured out 'the sex,' but did you do it safely?"

"Apparently not, Gran! I'm pregnant!"

"Well, at least let me talk to you about STDs then."

"La, la, la!" I sing and stick my fingers in my ears.

Not one to be deterred, she speaks louder. "Let's see, what are the biggies...?" She taps her chin with her finger. "Ooh, gonorrhea! That's a good one. Yes, you've got to avoid gonorrhea. What's another one...?" More thoughtful taps on her chin. "Genital warts! Genital warts are very bad stuff. And from what I understand, the clap is just terrible too."

I'm not sure why I'm engaging in this, but...

"Actually, Gran, the clap *is* gonorrhea. They're the same thing."

"Really? I always assumed the clap was chlamydia."

"Well, it's not. It's gonorrhea."

She looks at me with affection. "My granddaughter is so smart. Now, why do you suppose it's called the clap, sweetheart?"

This is certainly not the conversation I thought I'd be having tonight.

I pop a grape in my mouth. "Actually, there are different theories about that. One theory is that in the early days of gonorrhea treatment, people would literally clap the penis to try to expel the disease."

"Oh dear!" Gran winces.

"I know, right? Some of the other theories have to do with etymology. The French word clapier means brothel—a place where many STDs were transmitted back in the day. And clappan is an old English word that means to beat or throb. It describes the pain of the gonorrhea itself."

Gran's brow furrows. "May I ask why you know so much about this subject?"

"Don't worry, Gran. I've never run into trouble on that front." I shrug. "You know me. I was an English major. I love words."

"So… how's your writing coming?"

Smooth, Gran, smooth.

"Gran." I give her a look.

"What? You mentioned how much you love words. It was an excellent segue for me to ask you about your writing."

I sigh. "You know as well as anyone that I don't write anymore."

"And why not? You're a wonderful writer. When you were a little girl, you wrote book after book after book. Oh, the adventures that got left on my kitchen table every day for me to read. They were delightful. *You* are a delightful writer. You should keep writing."

"Yeah, well, I tried."

"When did you try?" Gran asks slyly.

"In college! I tried writing children's books, but – "

"But what?"

"The inspiration just wasn't there anymore." I shrug. "Besides, Gran, it's hard to make decent money as a writer."

"Who cares about money? Money's not important."

"That's a bold statement coming from a woman whose farm is still deep in the red," I say and instantly regret it when her features fall ever so slightly.

"Slowly but surely, we're figuring that out, aren't we?" she says firmly. "The Bedd family always finds a way."

"Yeah." I rub the tense spot gathering between my eyebrows. "We do."

"So?" She taps the table again. "When can we expect another tale from the great Colleen Murphy Bedd?"

I sigh. "Gran, I'm better off *reading* books to kids, not writing them."

"I just think if you put yourself out there again, you could—"

My chair screeches when I abruptly rise from the table. "I appreciate your thoughts, Gran, but I don't want to talk about this anymore." I rinse my empty bowl and place it gently in the dishwasher.

"Alright then." She gives up for now, but I know this won't be the last I hear on the subject. She moves to the stove and fires up the kettle. "I, for one, would like another cuppa. To return to our earlier conversation, don't you think chlamydia sounds like an herbal tea? It's way too pretty a name for a sexually transmitted disease that causes painful urination."

I have to laugh at that. "You have a point there, Gran."

"Care to join me for a cup of chlamydia tea?" she asks innocently.

I smile. "I'd love to, but I'm suddenly feeling really tired, so I'm going to head back up to bed."

"Alright, sweetheart. You get some rest. Growing a baby is

serious work. Thanks for spending a little time with me. You know I love our kitchen chats."

"I do too, Gran."

So much.

"Turn the lights back out on your way up, will you?" she asks as she settles back into her seat, waiting for the water to boil.

I do as she asks, plunging the kitchen back into darkness. I stand in the doorway until my eyes adjust, and I can make out her small frame sitting at the table.

"Can I ask what this whole sitting in the dark thing is about?"

"This is what I always do when I'm waiting for one of my kids to come home," she says, as if it's common Bedd knowledge. "Everything is more peaceful in the dark. That's when all the farm night noises perk up. The bugs, the frogs in the creek, the coyotes on the mountains. The critters are all a little quiet in the wintertime, but if you listen real close, you can hear them."

I rest against the doorframe in silence and listen. Sure enough, a coyote howls from a distance.

"See?" she says proudly, then hums a little tune.

Something is different about Gran tonight. She seems dreamy? Possibly a little foggy? Maybe it's because I lost my parents young, or perhaps it's because my brain needs something to worry about, but all it takes is one hint that my grandmother's mind could be failing her, and I leap into investigative mode.

"Gran." I speak slowly. "I've been in my room for the past hour. And the boys don't live here anymore…"

"I know that." She chuckles.

"Well, you just said you were waiting for one of your kids to come home, so I thought maybe you'd gotten a little confused."

She scoffs. "I'm sharp as a tack, missy, and you know it. I was talking about your beau."

"You're waiting up for Bacon?"

She already considers him one of her kids?

"Do you have another beau I'm not aware of?" she asks. "I'm trying to keep up with the times, Colleen, but my goodness, you're asking a lot of an old woman all at once."

I chuckle in the dark. "No, Gran. Bacon is my only beau."

"That's good." She gets up when the kettle squeals. "Don't get me wrong, if you told me you were throupling now and you had a boyfriend named Beef and another named Tenderloin, I would find a way to accept and support it. I dip into those spicy books you leave around the house, and I've learned a thing or two. What is it called when ladies have several fellas? 'Don't pick?'"

"Why choose," I gently correct. "Not to get technical, but the example you just gave would be considered a quad."

"A what?" She pours her tea.

"Beef, Bacon, Tenderloin, and I wouldn't be a throuple. We'd be a quad."

"I see. Well, regardless, I would support the love you four found together."

"You really would, wouldn't you?" I say, somewhat in awe of all the changes Gran has made this year. If a woman in her early seventies can keep learning and growing, maybe there's hope for me too.

She moves to where I'm standing in the doorway and places a warm, weathered hand on my cheek. "All I want is for my grandchildren… " She moves her hand to my belly. "…and my great-grandchildren to be happy."

"Thanks, Gran. I love you."

"I love you too, sweet girl. We don't say that enough in our family, do we?"

"No, I guess we don't." I hesitate, not sure I should say

what wants to come out of my mouth next. "You know who else told me they love me tonight?"

"Who, dear?"

"Bacon."

"Well, isn't that lovely," she says softly.

"I think he was drunk, and he told me over text, so I don't know if that counts, but—"

"It counts." Gran nods. "And it's lovely."

"You don't think it's too soon?" I ask, my voice sounding like a little kid's, even to my own ears.

"Too soon for what?" she says. "For love? I've never understood these arbitrary rules people place on relationships. 'You should wait at least one month before saying 'I love you.' You should date for at least six months before getting engaged. You should be engaged at least a year before you're married.' Should, should, should. Can we all stop should-ing on ourselves? It's all nonsense."

"Aren't you the woman who said 'rules are rules for a reason' on repeat throughout my entire childhood?" I laugh.

"I am that woman," Gran says. "But know this, Colleen Murphy Bedd, rules apply to farm chores and curfews. Rules never apply to love."

Having said her piece, she shuffles back to the table to enjoy her tea while I head back upstairs, my heart fuller than it's been in weeks.

I may not be ready to say those three words back to Bacon yet, but one thing is certain: I love my Gran to the moon and back.

I don't know what I'd do without her, and I hope it's a really long time before I have to find out.

CHAPTER 18
BACON

I SLOWLY CREEP THROUGH THE KITCHEN DOOR OF COLLEEN'S gran's house, trying not to wake anyone.

I almost have a heart attack when someone says, "How was the titty bar, dear?"

Ethel Bedd sits in the dark kitchen, wearing the same red-and-white-striped pajamas as I am.

"Wow!" I say, my heart pounding. "There you are! Hello! I mean, good evening, Mrs. Bedd. Did I—did I—I'm sorry, did I wake you?"

"Not at all. I'm what they call a night owl. Hoot, hoot! Did you have fun with the boys? Tell me about your titty time."

"We had... a lot of fun. But, ma'am..." I swallow. "I think you mean Tiddy's? As I learned tonight, it's a double D, not a double T."

"Ah, I remember when I had double Ds," she says wistfully.

Am I supposed to respond to that?

Apparently, I am because the sweet woman is staring at me expectantly.

"What, um, what happened to them?" I try desperately not to cast my eyes anywhere in the vicinity of her chest.

"Breastfeeding happened, dear. Don't tell Colleen this, but breastfeeding can suck the life right out of a lady's titties."

"Mrs. Bedd, would it be okay if neither of us said titties again in each other's presence?"

"Oh, of course. Your generation is all about setting boundaries, right?"

"I guess so?"

"I can respect that. No more tittie talk." She waves her hands and moves toward the hallway. Let's get you upstairs. I set you up a little Bedd bed in my husband's old office. I would gladly offer you the spare bedroom or the attic, but we've had WWOOFers staying with us. They're away briefly for the holidays but left their things in their rooms, and I'd rather not violate their privacy."

"You've had dogs staying with you?"

"No, dear." She chuckles. "WWOOFers. It stands for Worldwide Opportunities on Organic Farms. Folks volunteer on farms like ours in exchange for free room and board."

"Ah, I see." I follow her up a creaky set of stairs and whisper, "I was hoping to talk to Colleen. Is she already asleep?"

"I think you were hoping to share a bed with Colleen," she whispers back saucily.

"No, ma'am. Not at all."

"I know it seems silly having you two sleep separately when you've already made a baby together, but I have to hang on to at least a *few* of my old-fashioned beliefs. Hard as I try to get rid of them, those pesky 'what will the neighbors think' thoughts still swim around in my mind from time to time."

"I completely understand."

"Though I *did* let it slide when Sam and Diane were getting cozy under my roof not too long ago," Colleen's grandmother continues. "But those kids needed a little push in the right direction. Let's just say I take these matters on a case-by-case basis."

"You don't owe me any explanation, ma'am. This is your home. I will gladly abide by your rules."

"Such a nice boy."

We reach the top of the steps, and she ushers me through an open door. "Here we are. I blew up this very uncomfortable air mattress for you and placed your suitcase in that small closet. Bathroom is right down the hall and should have everything you need. Convenient that you're already in your jammies too, isn't it?"

"It is. Thank you for including me in your new family tradition. I have to say, you look adorable in those holiday jammies, Mrs. Bedd."

"Thank you, sweetheart. When you have a figure like mine, you might as well flaunt it, I always say!"

"*Do* you always say that?" I ask. It seems a little out of character for the woman Colleen has described.

"Well, I do now," she explains. "I'm in the era of trying new things. Give me a follow on TikTok, and you'll see what I mean!"

"Ha! I will definitely do that."

I take a moment to scan the room. It's an office from another era. And it's frozen in time. A wooden desk sits under a window with an old calculator and reams of lined yellow paper at the ready, like the man who ran this farm will be back any minute to resume his work and calculations. The metal bookshelf to the left is bursting with binders labeled Bedd Fellow Farms, with bright green stickers showcasing the year. As far as I can tell, they're not organized into any cohesive pattern. Binders from 1998 are wedged against ones from 1987. A few from the late seventies are even mixed in.

It saddens me to think about Colleen's grandfather up in this office at night, desperately crunching numbers and keeping all the details to himself. The stress he was carrying must have been enormous.

That stress has now been passed on to his wonderful family, and I really want to find a way to help.

"This is wonderful. Thank you, Mrs. Bedd."

"Please. Call me Ethel."

"I couldn't."

"You can and you will," she insists.

"Isn't that a little—I don't know—disrespectful?"

She sighs. "What I wouldn't give for a man to disrespect me right now."

"Excuse me?" I say and immediately regret it. "Excuse me" implies I want Colleen's seventy-one-year-old grand-mother to repeat what she just said, and I very much do not want that to happen.

"Well, Bacon, when I said 'what I wouldn't give for a man to disrespect me right now,' what I meant was that I'd dearly like to have intercourse again."

"Mm. I see." That is all I can manage to say.

"Was that shocking, dear?"

"Not shocking," I say. "A little surprising, maybe?"

"Young people need to get with the program. Life doesn't end when you turn sixty," she huffs.

"I'm sure it doesn't," I say emphatically, hoping I haven't offended her.

"I'll have you know, Bacon—this might surprise you too, but—when I saw you on that television screen, my very first thought was, 'well, that there is a very sexy boy.'"

"Oh, that's—That's, uh—"

"Completely natural, that's what that is." She turns even more serious than she already was. "But I've put those feel-ings behind me now that you've impregnated my grand-daughter. It's the right thing to do. I wouldn't want there to be any awkwardness between us."

"Yes. Awkwardness would be terrible." I look frantically around the room for something to spark a subject change. A framed family photo catches my attention. "May I?" I ask as I reach for it.

"Of course," Ethel says. "Colleen and Samuel were around eleven there. That was just about one year after their parents passed.

"She was adorable," I say in an almost whisper.

The photo gives me a glimpse of what our little girl or boy could look like a decade from now. I'm struck by how young and innocent she was. By the sweet smile on her face, in spite of everything she'd already been through.

I don't know how long I'm lost in the photo before Mrs. Bedd says softly, "Did she not respond to your drunken declaration of love this evening?"

Now that my beer buzz is wearing off, I'm keenly aware of the fact that I sent Colleen impromptu poetry that went completely unanswered.

"She did not," I say on a heavy exhale.

"I wouldn't worry about that, sweetheart. I can tell you're the kind of spirited boy who dives into life whole hog, but my girl takes her time. Especially with her heart." She reaches a hand up and pats my shoulder. "I hope you'll be patient with her."

"I'll give that woman whatever she needs," I say, carefully placing the photo back on the desk.

Colleen's grandmother responds with a warm smile and a pinch to my cheek.

"Thank you for welcoming me so generously into your home. You didn't have to be so understanding and accommodating, yet you are." I clear my throat. "It, um. It feels important to assure you that I do not make a habit of 'diving into life penis first.' The connection I felt with your granddaughter was so intense, so immediate… well, I guess we lost track of ourselves that day. But I can't feel an ounce of regret for that because I found something I never knew I was missing." I take a deep breath in, then let it out. "I love her, Mrs. Bedd."

"I know you do, sweetheart." She points at my face. "It's in the eyes. Always in the eyes." She makes her way to the door, gives me a wink, and says, "Sleep tight now, son."

Son. No one's ever called me that before.

"Sleep tight, Ethel," I say and fight the urge to go all misty-eyed. What a day this has been. One for the record books, for sure.

Once I'm alone, I clean up in the small bathroom down the hall, then spend way too much time standing outside Colleen's closed bedroom door contemplating knocking or just slipping inside. But I don't want to wake her. Plus, I just finished telling her grandmother I respect her rules and we'd sleep separately. I'm not going to damage all that goodwill we've established by going against Ethel's wishes.

But damn, I want to hold her.

Colleen, that is. Not her grandmother. One would think that'd be obvious, but it doesn't hurt to be specific after the conversation that veered on flirtation just now.

Maybe I shouldn't have gone out with Colleen's brothers tonight. When they invited me out after dinner, she said she was cool with it and that I should go, but after four months apart from her, I should be soaking up every minute we have together, not trying to fit in with "the cool kids."

I have to hand it to them, though. The Bedd brothers really are cool. They seem so confident in who they are in the world and who they are to each other. I don't doubt they've had their struggles over the years, but seeing them now as grown men busting on each other, talking shit... it all seems so comforting. Having a shared history with siblings is something I've always craved. It was nice for one night being welcomed into their fold.

Returning to my temporary bedroom, I strip down to my boxer briefs, slip on a tee shirt, and lie down on the air mattress.

"It's squeaky, isn't it?"

The voice I'd know anywhere sounds through the wall.

I turn my head toward the mint green wallpaper. "Colleen?"

"These walls are incredibly thin," she says. "How was the night?"

"It was fun. But I was just thinking, I should've stayed here with you. I'm sorry. I know you have feelings like people favor your brothers over you, and I'd never want you to think—"

"That you favor my brothers over me?"

"Yeah," I say, realizing how ridiculous that sounds now that I've said it out loud.

"I would never think that. I mean, would my brothers play *Yes, Chef!* with you on your marble countertop and let you knock them up on the first date?"

"No. No, they would not."

"Exactly. I'm not worried. You know where your bread is buttered." She laughs softly.

"Do you think we'll… butter bread together again at some point?" I ask like an idiot.

"I certainly hope so. It won't be tonight, though. Gran's orders."

"Yes. Gotta respect Gran's orders."

"And you gotta stop flirting with my grandmother."

"Flirting with your grandmother? What are you even—"

"'I have to say, you look adorable in those holiday jammies, Mrs. Bedd.'" She does a damn good impression of me. "Like I said, these walls are thin."

"For the record, I was not flirting with her," I say. "I was simply appreciating a beautiful woman who has always taken care of *my* beautiful woman."

"I'm your beautiful woman, huh?" she says playfully.

Did I take that too far?

"Yes? But, of course, I mean that in a fully feminist, nonpossessive, I-know-you-are your-own-person and I-am-my-own-person kind of way."

"I loved your text," she says, shocking the hell out of me.

"You did? When you didn't respond, I assumed you thought it was weird."

"Oh, it was hella weird. The weirdest!" she confirms. "But do you remember what I said all those months ago back in your apartment? I like my guys with a touch of weird."

"That's a singular guy now, right? Not to get nitpicky, but back then, you said you like your *guys*—plural—with a touch of weird."

"There's really only one guy I want these days," she says, and I've never wished I could be in the same room with someone more.

"That's good," I say. "Because there's only one woman I want and—"

"I'm not ready to say 'I love you' yet, Bacon. You should know that."

I nod in the dark even though she can't see me.

"Totally understand. Colleen, that's not why I said it—"

"You said it because you were drunk," she gently accuses.

"No," I say firmly. "I said it because I meant it. Correction: I *mean* it. And I don't expect anything back. I promise."

"I like you so much it scares me." She pauses. "That's what I can say."

"Works for me, Chef. I'm scared too."

"You are?" Her voice pitches upward, like my admission delights her. "Wait, why did you call *me* Chef?"

"In restaurants, it's customary for everyone working in the kitchen to call each other chef. Shows that we're all on the same team."

"Oh," she breathes.

"You and I? We're on the same team now."

"I like the sound of that," she says and lets out a yawn.

"So do I." I curl up on my side, still staring at the wall,

wishing we were face-to-face. "By the sounds of it, we should let you get some sleep."

"Do you have plans in the morning?" she asks.

"Lady, my only plan is you."

"Okay. Because I made myself an OB-GYN appointment tomorrow morning to confirm the pregnancy and have my first ultrasound."

"Wow. That's really—"

"Will you come with me?" she asks.

"Colleen, nothing would make me happier."

"Great," she says, and I can hear the smile in her voice, even through this farmhouse wall. "Good night, Chef."

"Good night, Chef."

CHAPTER 19
COLLEEN

I'M SITTING ON A MEDICAL TABLE, NAKED FROM THE WAIST DOWN, with only a thin paper sheet covering my lap and feeling equal parts anxious and excited.

"Pretty odd situation for a third date, huh?" I joke.

"I've had odder," Bacon says.

"You have?"

He picks up a life-size anatomical model of the female pelvis and makes it talk in a high, squeaky voice. "Actually, no, I have not."

"Oh my god, stop." I laugh. "Women do not sound like that. And get your hands off that lady's butt bones!"

"Lady, these are not butt bones. They are pubic bones—"

"Bleh. I hate the word *pubic*."

"Love it or hate it, Colleen, these *pubic* bones are pretty amazing. Did you know they actively spread apart during labor to allow the baby to move through the birth canal?" He accompanies this fact with a demonstration, repeatedly spreading the bones with his hands. "See? In and out. In and out."

"Knock, knock!" a melodic voice calls out, and a woman in teal scrubs enters the room. She's instantly familiar to me, but I can't place her. Bacon catches her attention first. "Sir.

Please don't manhandle the female pelvis." He's about to apologize when she lowers her voice to a faux seductive tone and says, "Unless we ask you nicely, that is."

"Um…" That's all Bacon manages to say in response.

"But seriously, sir. Put the anatomical model down. That shit is expensive."

He puts the pelvis back on its metal stand.

The woman plops onto a plush rolling stool and wheels a white machine in my direction. She takes one look at me and squeals.

"Colleen Bedd! As I live and breathe!"

She launches from her seat to give me a tight hug, sending the rolling stool careening across the room. I wasn't planning on hugging a woman today while half naked, but as I've learned, life is full of surprises.

"Hi, um—uh…" I stammer.

I give her a few pats on the back while it comes back to me. We went to middle school together. She was the one who started the "Elizabethans for Ethan" club. Then she moved away soon after. Why can't I remember her name? It's on the tip of my tongue…

"Melinda!" she says, breaking the hug and placing a palm on her chest.

"Right! Yes! Of course. Hi, Melinda. What are you, uh, what are you doing here? I haven't seen you since, gosh, seventh grade?"

"I know, I know, I know." She waves a hand in the air. "My parents' divorce meant I had to leave Fork Lick for Ohio, which was the worst. I got married and started my own family there—bloom where you're planted and all, right?— but now *I'm* the one getting a divorce, so *I* get to decide where *I* wanna live. I moved back to Fork Lick with my kids just last week, and now I'm one of the new ultrasound techs here at Climax OB-GYN." She giggles. "Gosh, I don't know if I'll ever get used to saying that. I don't like all the silly jokes about

Climax, but when you put that word next to OB-GYN, it really does sound scandalous, doesn't it? I'm sorry to disappoint you, Colleen, but we keep things strictly professional at this establishment. Hence, no climaxes will be doled out today at this here doctor's appointment."

I look at Bacon. His eyes are wide, and his mouth is slightly open.

"I'm not disappointed, Melinda. And gosh, I should hope not!"

Melinda's face turns serious. "How are your handsome brothers doing? I mean, they were gorgeous when they were in middle school and high school. They must all be sex on a stick now, huh?"

With that, she pulls out an actual stick. A bulbous white stick that she promptly covers with a condom.

What in the world is that?

"Any of them single?" She continues and points at herself with the unknown medical object. "Because this lady is officially single and ready to mingle."

"I'd prefer if we didn't talk about my brothers right now if that's okay with you. Also, what the hell are you holding?"

"You're right, you're right. We're here to talk about you! Congratulations on your pregnancy by the way! *This*," Melinda says proudly, "is a transvaginal ultrasound wand."

"A transvaginal whatta-wand?" My voice pitches higher.

Melinda repeats. "A transvaginal ultrasound wand."

"That monstrosity is going inside me?" I squeak.

Melinda nods. "It is! Isn't that exciting?"

I look at Bacon for help. He places his hands on my shoulders and jokes with Melinda, who is still wielding this massive tool in my direction. "Transvaginal, huh?"

"Great word, right?" She giggles.

"For sure. Great word. Though, doesn't transvaginal sound like Colleen's lady parts are about to take the trip of a lifetime?"

"Well, they are!" Melinda beams. "Childbirth will spread Colleen's vagina's horizons further than she ever dreamed possible."

"Alright," I say, reaching for my pants. "I'm outta here."

Bacon gently stops me and stays on task. "It's Melinda, right?" he says.

"That's right."

"I feel like part of your job as an ultrasound technician should be to put patients—specifically first-time mothers—at ease. Would you agree?"

"Absolutely!"

"Great," Bacon continues. "I'm thinking that telling a woman how far her vagina is going to stretch in childbirth *might* not be the best way to ease her into her first OB-GYN appointment."

"Well, it's just a fact, Daddy. I don't think it's appropriate to sugarcoat the sheer carnage that comes with—"

He holds up a hand to silence her. "Understood, but this is essentially day one for us. Let's take things step by step, shall we? Starting with this ultrasound." He gestures to the condom-covered wand. "It's my understanding that the transvaginal wand is mostly used during the first trimester when the baby is very small, correct?"

"That's correct."

How does he know this?

"We're estimating that Colleen is already over four months along, well into her second trimester, so wouldn't it be just as effective to do an abdominal ultrasound at this point?"

"I suppose so."

"Terrific. Let's do that, then. If we spot anything that needs a closer look—not that we will—we can discuss returning to the... transvaginal option. Sound good?"

"Fine by me." She shrugs. She strips the wand of the condom and puts her weapon away.

Harold "Bacon" Hotman is my hero.

Melinda gets back to business. "Alright, girlfriend. Lie back for me and lift your shirt."

I do as she asks. She tucks a thin paper sheet into the waistband of my pants—to protect the fabric I suppose—and whips out a clear plastic bottle filled with greenish-blue gel.

"This will feel a little cool on your skin," she warns, squeezing a little gel heart pattern around my belly button.

"Wow!" I chuckle. "A heart, huh?"

"Just a little love squirt." She giggles and squeezes another heart on my abdomen. "I like to go the extra mile with my patients. I figure a little love squirt got you two into this situation, right?" She turns to Bacon. "Just think, Daddy, if you'd squirted on her belly like I just did, things may have turned out differently for ya."

"Melinda?" Bacon says with total calm.

"Yes, Daddy."

He catches himself mid-sigh, then continues. "I'd be okay if you never said love squirt to me again. And please don't call me Daddy. Bacon is fine."

"Really?" she whines. Something tells me that calling soon-to-be fathers "Daddy" during ultrasound appointments is the highlight of her day. "Alright," she acquiesces. "Bacon it is." She holds up a far less intimidating tool than the one she had before. "Are we ready for a sneaky peeky at your baby?"

"I think so?" I take a deep breath and hold it.

I look up at Bacon, standing beside me. He responds by interlacing his fingers with mine and flashing me that beautiful smile.

"We're ready," he says.

Melinda places the tool on my belly and swirls it around a few times over the gel. "Just a little pressure…"

And then the most beautiful image I've ever seen appears on the screen.

"That's our baby," I whisper.

Bacon's hand squeezes mine tighter.

Melinda points at the screen with one hand as she continues light pressure with the other. "That there is the head. The arms... the legs. Aw, a cute little baby bum. And you see that flicker in the center right there? That's the heart."

That rhythmic flutter on the screen literally takes my breath away. Time stops. My own heart flutters like it's in conversation with the tiny little heart forming inside me. When I finally remember to pull in a lungful of air, I hear a sniffle from the man beside me.

One salty tear rolls down Bacon's cheek.

The expression on his face can only be described as awe.

The man is in love.

But with our baby this time. It's beautiful to see.

Melinda's all business now while she types notes into her computer. "You two were correct. Baby is measuring at around sixteen weeks, which brings your due date to... May twentieth."

"That was my mom's birthday," I say in wonder.

"Aw, what a sweet coincidence!" Melinda says.

But I'm not so sure I believe in coincidences anymore. I didn't see any of this coming, yet somehow, it all feels meant to be. Suddenly, it's like every single thing I've experienced—the good and the terrible—has led me here to this moment with this beautiful man. As someone who lost her parents when she was ten years old, the whole "everything happens for a reason" mentality has always felt like a slap in the face. But I'm starting to think it might be true. If I hadn't gone to New York City that day... If I hadn't missed the bus home... Hell, if I hadn't had that awkward run-in with my student at the Quick Lick and been forced to buy a pack of primary-colored washable markers... none of this would be happening right now.

I lock eyes with Bacon and squeeze his hand. "I'm so happy," I say, my voice breaking on the last word.

"Never been happier in my whole life," he responds, eyes still glistening. He leans over me on the table, places his warm hand on my cheek, and kisses me. I get lost in the kiss. It's probably too intimate a kiss to be sharing with another person in the room, but honestly, I forget Melinda's even there until I hear her say...

"Oop!"

Bacon pulls back from the kiss. "Oop?" he says. "What does oop mean?"

"It means someone was hiding in there."

My adrenaline spikes. "Who was hiding where?" I prop myself on my elbows and crane my neck past Bacon to see the screen.

Melinda points at one image on the monitor and says, "This is Baby A." She points at *another* and says, "And this is Baby B. Congratulations, Mommy and Daddy. You're having twins."

Twenty minutes later, we're both still in shock.

After Melinda dropped the news that we're having twins—two whole babies!—she left, and I met my new OB. He examined me, told me all about prenatal vitamins, and confirmed that I should come back next month for my twenty-week scan. This is the "fun" anatomy scan where the ultrasound tech studies the various systems. We'll get a front-row seat to study the babies' hearts, brains, spines, stomachs, and lungs. We can even find out the sex of the babies if we want.

We're alone now in the exam room but I haven't moved yet to get dressed.

"Do you, uh—do you want to know if they're boys or girls?" I say softly. "Or one of each maybe?"

"Totally up to you. I'll be thrilled however things line up, and it'll be an awesome surprise whenever we find out, whether at the twenty-week scan or at the birth itself."

"Really? You'll be thrilled no matter what?"

"Of course," he says.

"You don't have hopes of having two boys?"

Bacon shrugs. "Not particularly."

I narrow my eyes at him. "Doesn't every man want sons? My dad certainly did. My grandad always seemed more invested in the boys too."

He tilts his head to the side and gives me a small smile. "May I?" He gestures to the exam table, where I sit with a paper sheet over my lap.

I move over and pat the space next to me. He sits, and I snuggle up close beside him. He puts his arm around me and pulls me even closer.

His voice is soft and gentle when he says, "I feel sorry for any of the men in your life who made you feel like you weren't a top priority. If they couldn't see how strong and smart and hilarious you are? Well, then, they were idiots. Because you, Colleen Bedd, are incredible."

"Aw," I say and drop my head on his shoulder.

"I'm serious, Colleen." He turns his head and kisses my hair.

Has anyone ever kissed my hair?

"Thank you. You're very sweet. But maybe we shouldn't call my deceased father and grandfather idiots?" I half laugh, half cringe.

He nods. "My apologies. I retract the insensitive name-calling but not the sentiment itself. Your dad and grandad missed out."

"Don't get me wrong, they were both good men. They worked hard, and they provided. But I guess I never felt like they wanted to *know* me." I pause. This is the first time I've expressed this stuff out loud. It feels disrespectful somehow. "Am I making any sense?"

"More than you know." Bacon clears his throat. "Colleen. I'm aware that our relationship so far has been—" He stops himself abruptly. "Are you comfortable with me calling this a relationship? I know you want to take things slow."

"When did I ever say I want to take things slow?" I laugh.

"Last night you said—"

"I said I'm not ready to say I love you, but Bacon, I'm pregnant with *two* of your children. My family threw you a pork party. We're most definitely in a relationship, and nothing about it is slow."

"Can I ask your opinion on something?" he says tentatively. He looks more nervous than he did on the *Yes, Chef!* stage.

"You're not asking me to marry you, are you?" I panic slightly.

"My, my, we're confident, aren't we?" he jokes.

My cheeks turn pink. "I'm sorry, I didn't mean to be—"

"Colleen Bedd, I'd marry the shit out of you right now—today—if you'd let me. But I know you're not ready for that. I was thinking, though… we should talk about where we're going to live."

Before Bacon came back to the house last night—and before my chat with Gran—I'd been staring at the glow-in-the-dark star stickers on my bedroom ceiling, wondering how we would make this all work. He's supposed to open a successful restaurant in a big city in the next few months. And, as much as I craved a day to be wild and anonymous in Manhattan, my home is here in Fork Lick. I don't want to leave Gran and my pain-in-the-butt brothers. I have sisters-in-law now too, for all intents and purposes, and I love them to bits. I feel like we're moving into The Bedd Family Version 2.0. We're growing, and not just in size, but emotionally too. Ethan and Alex have buried the hatchet, so to speak. Sam is discovering himself more and more every day, which, as his sister, is a thrill to see. The Bedd Family is finally finding our footing together, and I don't want to miss a minute of it.

It's a huge relief when Bacon says...

"What if I relocate to Fork Lick?"

"You'd do that?" I breathe. "What about your place in Philadelphia? What about your plans for the restaurant?"

"Once the show ended, my plan was to head back to Philly and the restaurant where I've been working for years. But I didn't expect to win, you know?" He chuckles. "I get to open my own restaurant now, so I called my old boss and let him know my temporary leave would be permanent. And I'm month to month with my landlord in Philly. I'll email him this afternoon and give my notice too. There's a whole world to explore and I'm ready to explore it."

"You could go anywhere on the planet, and you're choosing Fork Lick of all places?" I marvel.

"I'm choosing you and our babies."

Sweeter words were never spoken.

He takes my face in both hands and kisses me. I melt into him for all of five seconds before I break the kiss and ask again, "But what about your plans for the restaurant? The producers won't allow you to open in a tiny town like Fork Lick."

"Actually, they will," he says. "I got on a call with them this morning. They think it's a great idea. The concept is comfort food, right? What's more comforting than a small town packed with family and friends?"

"Careful what you wish for, sir, those family and friends will be all up in our business 24/7. I bet Melinda is already tagging everyone I went to middle school with to tell them about the Bedd Babies about to be born out of wedlock."

"Wedlock, schmedlock," he says, waving a hand.

"Wedlock, schmedlock, huh?" This man makes me laugh. "Is that a technical term?"

"It is. Let people talk. And as for family getting up in our business? That's already working in our favor. Last night, Sam mentioned that white church that borders your farm. He said it's newly vacant and could make a great space for the restaurant. I checked out the photos online, and I think the choir loft could even be converted into a living space for us and the babies."

"You already reached out to the real estate agent, didn't you?" I ask.

He winces. "I did. I sent an email and cc'd the show producers. We can check it out today if you're interested. It's kind of perfect, but I won't pull the trigger on it until I have your okay."

"*You're* perfect," I say.

Where did this man come from? He factors my feelings into every decision he makes. He's thoughtful and funny. He's resourceful, strong, and kind, and I'm thrilled he's mine.

"Remember last night when you asked when we could butter bread together again?" I ask.

"Yes?"

"How does right now hit you?" I say, a husk lilt in my tone.

"Right here? In this doctor's office?"

"If you're not in the mood, we could always wait another four months…" I tease and reach for my pants.

"You leave those pants right where they are," he says, very bossy all of a sudden. "Know this, woman, I'm never *not* in the mood to butter your bread."

After a quick dash to the door to secure the lock, he tears off his pants and kneels on the linoleum floor, settling himself between my bare thighs. "I know the clock's ticking, but you didn't let me linger here last time. Will you let me linger, beautiful?"

What in the world can a girl say to that?

He dives into my center like a man starved. He licks,

savors, and hums. "You're the most delicious thing I've ever tasted," he says between tongue strokes.

True to his word, he lingers. But within minutes, I'm climbing to my peak. Pleasure soars through me, pulsing over and over all the way down to my fingers and toes. I know we're skating on thin ice here. Someone could come to the door at any second, but I didn't wait four long months to touch this man again not to have him inside me.

"Get up here," I say when I've just barely caught my breath.

He's the one following orders now.

Somehow, Bacon makes mounting an exam table sexy. He fists his cock above me, and with one upward stroke, he's ready to go. "Condom? Do we need a condom?" he whispers.

"I haven't been with anyone since you," I whisper back.

"Same," he says with a smile.

"And I suppose you can't get me pregnant *twice*."

"Didn't I already get you pregnant twice?" he jokes.

"You know what I mean," I say. "No condom necessary."

"Excellent." He presses his length inside me inch by delicious inch until he's fully seated. "Heaven," he pants. "Holy shit, Colleen, you feel like heaven."

"You do too," I breathe.

"This will be fast," he warns.

"That's really our only option right now, sir."

"Still love when you call me 'sir,'" he says as he begins to thrust.

"Sir, Chef, Daddy... I'll call you whatever you want. Just keep fucking me."

The next few minutes are a blur of stifled moans and muffled cries as we chase our pleasure while simultaneously trying to avoid announcing the adult activities occurring in our exam room. Surely, this medical practice knows what got us into this position in the first place, but I doubt they'd appreciate us performing those activities in their place of business.

But right now, I can't bring myself to care.

"I'm close," I whisper. "So close."

"God, I love you, Colleen. I can't get close enough."

That's all it takes for us both to soar into the stratosphere.

A moment later, we lie tangled up in each other on a paper sheet.

"That. Was. Incredible." Bacon says, trying to catch his breath and failing.

Right as I'm about to say, "We really should get out of here," a light knock sounds on the door.

It's Melinda. "Seems I was wrong! Climaxes were doled out at this doctor's appointment after all. Ha ha. But, um, seriously, if you two are finished, we could really use this room for our next patient."

The whole office heard everything.

I should be embarrassed.

Humiliated even.

But for the first time in my life, I don't care what people think about me. I'm happy.

Like Bacon said, "Let them talk."

CHAPTER 20
BACON

IT'S BEEN SIX WEEKS SINCE OUR FIRST DOCTOR'S APPOINTMENT. I'm walking down the halls of Fork Lick Elementary with two things in my hands: the keys to our new home/restaurant and flowers for the girl of my dreams.

I'm starting to think that maybe life doesn't have to be so hard. I can see something, want something, and get it. I can meet an incredible woman, fall in love with her, and create a family with her. I can have the life I've always imagined.

It's the end of Colleen's workday, so I thought I'd surprise her with a visit. I was perfectly happy to wait in the school lobby for her, but the vice principal kindly ushered me to her classroom so I could greet her at her door.

She's finishing story time with her kindergarteners when I arrive. Not wanting to disturb her lesson or distract the kids, I stay in the hall and peek just past the open doorframe.

"Who can tell me the moral of the story we just read?" she asks sweetly. "Remember yesterday we talked about what a moral is? A moral is…"

"A lesson we can learn from a story," the kids answer in singsong unison.

"That's exactly right. What can we learn from *Penguin Problems* by Jory John? Yes. Jayden."

A boy with freckles and red hair answers, "Well, at first, the penguin was not happy. He was mad about all his problems. Like his beak was too cold, and the ocean was too wet, and all the penguins looked exactly the same, and no one knew who their parents were, and the sea creatures were always trying to eat him."

"That's true. He was only focused on the hard things in his life. But then what happened?" Colleen prompts. "Yes. Amaya."

A little girl with a jeweled bonnet says, "Well, he almost got eaten like a hundred times, but then he met this super nice walrus who speaks really fancy, and the walrus helps him see how beautiful the world is and how he's actually very lucky to be a penguin."

"Very good, Amaya. I love this book because it teaches us that problems are a part of life. They happen to everyone. Even cute little penguins like Mortimer. It's totally okay that Mortimer expressed all those grumpy feelings in the beginning of the book, right? We don't want to keep those feelings inside, but it's important to see the good parts of our lives too, like the warm sun on our feathers, the yummy food we get to eat, and the family and friends who love us. We'll never get rid of problems altogether, but if we're grateful for the good parts, things might just be okay."

A boy with silky black hair raises his hand. "Miss Bedd?"

"Yes, Simon."

"I agree with everything you just said except for the part about enjoying the sun on our feathers. I don't have feathers."

"You don't? I do!" Colleen jokes.

The kindergarteners squeal and laugh just as the bell rings, signaling the end of the day.

"Alright, everyone. You heard the bell. Please grab your backpacks from your cubbies and line up in the hallway. Our helper, Miss Kim, will take you out to the blacktop to meet your grown-ups. I'll see you tomorrow, friends!"

Colleen rises from the little reading stool where she sat and spots me. "What are you doing here?" she beams. God, she's beautiful. She's wearing a dark yellow dress with navy stripes, and at just over twenty weeks along, her belly is big and round now. The doctor told us with Colleen's small frame and the fact that she's carrying twins, we should expect her belly to grow fast. He wasn't kidding. And I love every second of it.

The kids scurry past me into the hallway, too excited about reuniting with their parents to pay me any attention.

"Good day, milady," I say and present the bouquet from behind me.

"You're so sweet." She double-checks that the kids are out of sight before giving me a soft kiss on the lips.

"That's not at all." I hold up the keys to our new space and dangle them midair.

"We're in?" she squeals.

"We're in. I am here to escort you there so I can officially carry you over the threshold." We hug, and one of the twins immediately gives a little kick. "Whoa! Getting strong in there, huh, kiddos?"

"You have no idea." Colleen sighs.

"Have I thanked you today for carrying our children?"

"You have," she says as she moves to the kids' painting station and fills a pitcher with water.

"And have I apologized for being such a large man, thus co-creating two large babies that will need to be birthed from your very small body?"

"Yes." She laughs. "You have."

I watch her arrange the flowers at her desk.

"You realize that was my first time seeing you teach?"

"Hm. I guess it would be. Were you positively dazzled?" she jokes.

"I was, actually! You're amazing with them."

She bats her hand in the air and stays focused on fixing the flowers.

"You are. And it gave me an idea."

"Oh yeah? What's that?"

"Teach cooking classes with me."

"What?"

"Teach cooking classes with me," I repeat. "It will be a few months until the restaurant can officially open and even longer until it starts turning a profit, but we can still bring in some money and press right now for your farm. Between my culinary skills and your teaching skills—not to mention your brilliance with lesson planning—we could create one hell of a cooking workshop for families. Parents, grandparents, and little kids all cooking together. How great would that be? We could do it on-site at the restaurant while it's still getting on its feet. All we need is a big, clean space, and we've got that. We can start promoting now and be operating within a month."

"How long have you been brainstorming this?" She chuckles and meets me in the center of the classroom.

"About five minutes. Brainstorm might not be accurate, though. It was more of a *lust* storm really."

"A lust storm, huh?" She lifts on her tiptoes and wraps her arms around my neck.

"Yeah." I rest my forehead against hers. "There's nothing sexier than seeing a woman totally in her element, doing what she was born to do."

"You think I was born to be a teacher?" she asks softly.

I think twice about what I just said and pull back slightly. "Weren't you? I mean, you're obviously incredible at it."

"Thanks," she says and moves to grab her purse from a cubby. "Yeah, thank you, that's, um. That's a huge compliment. Should we go? I'm curious to find out if you can still lift me for this threshold business."

"Hey. What's going on?" I meet her at the cubbies and intertwine our fingers. With my other hand, I tilt her chin up in my direction.

Her eyes are misty. "I love these kids. So much."

"I know you do. Anyone who sees you teach for two seconds knows you do."

She lowers her voice. "But I don't love the *job*." She hesitates. "I feel terrible saying that out loud, but it's true."

"Why do you feel terrible about that?"

"Because! I get to work with adorable children every day! I get to be part of setting them on a great educational path. I get to experience the magic of learning to read! Seriously, Bacon, you don't know real magic until you see everything click in a child's mind when they start to read."

Colleen's smile is wide, but there's still a well of sadness in her eyes.

I don't say anything. I just hold the space for her to continue.

She looks around her classroom. "I should be happy here. But I'm just… not. The pay is barely enough to get by month to month. The parents' demands are endless. The support we get from the district and the school board is virtually nonexistent." She pauses. "And now that these two are on the way…" When she rubs her belly, her eyes instantly brighten. "I can't imagine not being at home with them."

"Then stay home with them," I say before thinking. "I'll cover us financially."

"Us?" She sounds wary.

"Yeah, us," I say. "You, me, and our bacon bits."

"I don't want you to cover us financially," she says, an edge to her tone.

"Why not?"

"It's just not how I want to operate, Bacon. I think it's awesome for people if that's how their relationship works, but—" She shakes her head. "My grandad worshipped the ground Gran walks on, but I'm realizing how much he kept her in the dark about things. I guess they had a sort of unspoken agreement. She raised the kids. He took care of the business. When he passed, I had to watch her struggle to get a handle on her situation without him. And now, months later, I see Gran coming into her own. She's... blossoming. She's trying and experiencing things she'd never do if my grandfather were still here. My parents' relationship wasn't all that different when they were alive. The 'traditional' marriage arrangement works for some people, but it would never work for me."

"What are you saying? That you don't want to get married? That your grandmother would have been better off without your grandad?"

"*No.* None of that. I'm saying that I need to work. No matter what. And look, believe me, I know moms work. And as a mom of newborn twins, I will *really* be put to work, but it's vitally important to me that I do *my* work too."

"I get it. But..." I pause and try to figure out how to ask this next question delicately. "What *is* your work? You know, if teaching isn't ultimately what you want to do?"

There's a long moment of charged silence before she says, "Can I show you something?"

"Of course."

She moves to her desk and picks up a stack of papers bound together with a paper clip. Her eyes shine when she says, "Remember when I told you I was in publishing?"

"Yes?"

"That wasn't a lie." She interrupts herself when I cock my head in confusion. "Well, I guess it *was* a lie at the time, but I didn't want it to be. I wanted it to be true."

"Sorry, Colleen, I'm not following."

"I wrote a book!" She happily pats the bound papers in her hands.

"What?" I say in wonder.

"It's a children's book—a picture book—so it's short. But it's definitely a book! Oh my god, I wrote a book!"

She melts into my arms for a happy hug, pressing the papers between us.

I hold her close, still very confused. "When did you—How did you—Why didn't you tell me?"

"For the past six weeks, I've been working on it during every lunch break and free period. I didn't tell you because I wasn't sure I could do it. I've always wanted to be a writer, but I never let myself. Until now." She pulls back from the hug enough to look into my eyes. "You inspired me. I got a little nudge from Gran too."

"How did *I* inspire you?" I chuckle. "I've never written a damn thing."

"Maybe not, but you've been in constant creative mode since you decided to stay in Fork Lick. You're so lit up launching your restaurant. You found the perfect location. You're experimenting with dishes. You helped design the layout of the space." She shrugs. "Seeing that fire in you made me think... well, maybe there's a fire in me too."

"Oh, there's a fire in you, alright." I dive into her neck and cover her in kisses.

"Bay-CAHN." She giggles. "I'm at work."

"I was wondering when you were going to call me Bay-CAHN again." I land one more kiss, this time on her smiling lips. "Well? Let me see this thing." I reach for the papers.

She takes a step back, holding them out of my immediate reach. "You can't see it yet."

My eyebrows furrow. "A moment ago, didn't you literally say 'Can I show you something'?"

"I did. But I think I want you to wait until it's the real thing. I just printed these pages out on my own so I could feel them in my hands. The illustrations still need to be finalized and—"

"There are illustrations?"

"Of course!" she says. "It's a children's book! I reached out to an old friend from Vassar who works as an editor now. She taught me some of the basics of self-publishing, then connected me with this great illustrator, and it all sort of clicked. I mean, I obviously still have a lot to learn, but I'm really excited about everything."

"Amazing. What's the story about?"

She winces. "I think…"

"…you want me to wait until it's the real thing," I finish her sentence for her.

"Is that okay?"

"Of course it's okay. I love surprises. Surprise babies, surprise books… it's all very exciting. Who knows, maybe your book will hit it big and be the answer to Bedd Fellows' money troubles."

"Dare to dream." She sighs and tucks the manuscript safely in her desk drawer. "In the meantime, though, I like your idea. About the family cooking classes."

"You do?"

"Yeah." She smiles and grabs her purse. "I think we would make a pretty great team."

"We already do." I wrap an arm around her. "What do you say? Should we go check out our new digs? I don't know about you, but I'm getting a little bit tired of sneaking around behind Gran's back to get alone time with you. And speaking of backs, mine is killing me from six weeks on that air mattress. A brand-new king-sized bed with our name on it is being delivered to the new space as we speak."

"Oooh, sounds delightful." She flicks off the light switch as we exit the classroom together. "There *is* one more serious topic we need to discuss before we take any more big life steps together, though."

I take a deep breath and brace myself for the worst. "What is it?"

"A few minutes ago, did you call our unborn children *bacon bits*?"

"I did. What do you think?"

"I'm not sure how I feel about it for our children." She laughs. "But it would make an excellent name for a restaurant."

CHAPTER 21
COLLEEN

BBACON WAS RIGHT.

We are an excellent team.

After Bacon's brainstorm—or lust storm, as he called it—we spent a full month planning our family cooking workshops while I put the final touches on my book and sent it off for publishing. We created a menu and a curriculum. We sourced fresh ingredients from local Greene County farms and marketed our proverbial buns off. Fork Lick Elementary kindly included us in their monthly PTA newsletter. Molly emailed her CSA clients. Diane filmed a cute video interview with us and posted it on her YouTube channel. Gran's TikTok stardom continues to rise, and she used it to our advantage with several videos. The producing team at *Yes, Chef!* did a social media push for us too. Even Ginny offered to hang a poster up for us in The Quick Lick and include a flyer in every bag of groceries that leaves the store.

It feels like the entire town is showing us their support.

All the while, Bacon and I have been falling more and more in love up in the converted choir loft of our old white church while the design for the new restaurant takes shape below.

That's right.

I've fallen head over heels in love with him.

And today is the day I'm going to finally tell him.

We just wrapped our final class of the month-long family cooking workshops. It's unseasonably warm for early spring, so we're celebrating the end of the session today with a big spaghetti and meatball dinner out on our rolling farm hills— prepared by our students of course—followed by the ice cream we all made together by combining frozen Bedd Fellows Farm strawberries with the finest cream from Udderly Creamy.

I'm busy pulling tubs of ice cream out of the restaurant's massive freezers and placing them on a rolling cart when Ginny Quick wanders into the kitchen like she owns the place.

"Impressive showing today," she says, holding a bowl of spaghetti and munching on a meatball.

"Why, thank you, Gin. We're really proud of how every-thing turned out."

"You should be. You and Bacon brought in $32,000 this month for Bedd Fellows? That's incredible, Collie. It truly is."

"I appreciate that. And thanks for coming out today. It means a lot seeing how much the town has supported us."

"Oh, I wouldn't miss it." Ginny's eyes scan the restaurant space. She walks to the far end of the kitchen and peers up the back steps that lead to our loft. "It's ironic that a girl who can count the number of times she's been in a church on one hand is now living inside one," she says.

"Ha. True." I pull the last tub of ice cream out and place it on the rolling cart, readying to wheel it outside to our partici-pants. "To be fair, this building hasn't been a functioning church in over a decade."

It's true. Many businesses have tried and failed to succeed in this location over the years.

I really hope we're the business that sticks.

I hope *we* stick.

"You certainly have changed a lot over the years," Ginny says as she slurps a long piece of spaghetti into her mouth.

"How so?" I ask.

"Well, look at you! You're the girl who always said you were an 'independent woman.'"

"I *am* an independent woman," I say with no small amount of snark in my tone.

"Really?" Ginny's voice hits an irritating high note. "I don't mean any offense by this, and I'm over-the-moon happy for you, but your life looks anything but independent these days. In fact, I'd say it's downright dependent."

I should ask her to stop talking. I should politely tell her to leave. But apparently, I am a glutton for punishment because I say, "What do you mean?"

"When we were teenagers, you always said how much you hated the way your brothers controlled you—"

"Wait a minute," I interrupt her. "I don't think I said they *controlled* me—"

"You definitely did! You said they always had their noses in your business and didn't trust you to handle your 'own shit'—your words, not mine—and that when you were eighteen, you were going to live on your own and never let another man dictate what you do ever again."

"And I *don't* let men dictate what I do," I say firmly.

"You sure about that?" Impossibly, Ginny's tone inches even higher. "You said you wanted to be a writer, then boom! You accepted the first teaching job a man offered you."

"I was twenty-two years old. It was a decent-paying job for me at the time," I press. "And who cares if the person who hired me was a man or a woman?"

Ginny continues. "You said you wanted to live on your own, then boom! Your grandpa dies, and your brothers convince you to come back to Bedd Fellows to take care of Gran."

"They didn't *convince* me. I offered."

She's on a roll with her deconstruction of me, and she doesn't show any signs of stopping. "You said you wanted a fun day in the city, then boom—"

"Will you please stop saying boom!?" I plead, more exasperated by the minute.

"Boom! You get pregnant! Now here you are living with a man you barely know, supporting *his* restaurant dream, bearing *his* children, allowing *him* to make the decisions on how to save your family farm. You're basically living for *him*." Ginny finally pauses. She cocks her head to the side, studying me. "I dunno. It's just interesting."

"What's interesting?" a deep voice resonates from the doorway.

The "him" in question stands there looking as gorgeous as ever. But after Ginny's rant, I'm having a hard time looking at him.

I avert my eyes and catch my reflection in the shiny windows over the sink. Turns out I'm having a tough time looking at myself too.

Cautiously, Bacon asks, "What's going on, ladies?"

"Oh, nothing," Ginny says cheerfully. "Just girl talk. Is it time for the ice cream?"

Bacon's eyes are on me, but he responds slowly to Ginny. "Uh, yeah. That's what I was coming in to check on."

"Allow me!" Ginny chucks the last bit of her spaghetti bowl into the trash and takes hold of the ice cream cart. "I'm happy to wheel this baby around and serve everyone their ice cream."

"That's uh – that's very helpful, thank you," Bacon says, his eyes still trying to make contact with mine. "Sam and Diane are right outside. Alex and Molly too. They'll help you distribute to the participants."

"Not a problem," Ginny says. "Congrats on the successful venture, you two."

With that, she's gone.

But I'm standing here.

Still as a statue.

Not knowing who the hell I am anymore.

"What was that all about?" Bacon asks.

"Nothing," I say and finally surge into action, moving to the door. "We should get outside and help serve the ice cream. We're the ones running this thing and – "

He blocks my path to the door. "Colleen. What's going on? What just happened?"

"I told you. Nothing happened."

"So why do you look and sound so upset?" He places his warm hands gently on my shoulders.

"Can we just drop this, please?" I beg, fighting the tears forming in my eyes.

"Drop what? What are we dropping?"

I try to step around him. He doesn't let me go.

"Can you please move?" I demand.

"No," he says. "Not until you tell me what's going on."

"Oh, so now you control where I go and what I do?" I snap.

"What?" He lowers his hands from my shoulders. His voice softens to a near whisper. "When have I ever tried to control you?"

I shake my head. "You *haven't*. It's not you. It's me."

"Did you really just say 'it's not you, it's me'?"

I've let myself get so caught up in you, but still, I've let myself.

I finally allow myself to look into his eyes.

They're awash in confusion.

I feel terrible.

This isn't his fault.

But I know what I need to do.

He waits patiently for me to say something. I take a few moments to breathe. To gather my wits about me. Finally, I speak.

"I think I need to spend some time away from you."

He laughs. "Ha, good one."

"I'm serious."

His eyes narrow. "Where in the world is this coming from?"

"There are just some things I need to accomplish before the babies are born and the restaurant officially opens."

"Great." He reaches out and strokes my hair. "What are they? We'll accomplish them together."

"I don't want to accomplish them together. I need to be alone."

I see the moment panic rises in his body. "Colleen. Is everything okay? Are you and the babies okay?"

"Yes. We're great. I just—There's so much going on, and— I need some time to focus. On myself. In my whole life, I've never taken the time to truly focus on myself."

"And you can't focus on yourself with me?"

"No." I breathe. "I can't."

He stares out the window at the families happily eating the ice cream we taught them how to make. Alex's dog, Trixie, and Sam's dog, Gomer, lie lazily on the grass, letting playful children stroke their fur. Gran tells an animated story to three older gentlemen who seem utterly smitten by her charms. My siblings laugh and joke with the many friendly Fork Lickers who came out to support us today.

The world outside this building is teeming with life.

While the world *inside* feels like it's slowly dying.

When Bacon turns back to face me, a single tear rolls down his cheek.

There's only one thing I can think to say at this moment.

"I love you." Emotion clogs my throat. "This isn't the way I wanted to tell you for the first time, but it's true, Bacon. I love you so much it hurts."

"You love me," he says. "But you're leaving me." This time, his voice breaks. "Colleen, what happened? One minute, everything's fine. Amazing even! We're laughing, talking, planning our future together. Then, the next minute, you suddenly want to be alone and throw it all away?"

"Bacon, I still want to be with you. I'm just asking for time! And this isn't sudden. I've been worried for a while now about how fast everything is moving between us. We're like this—this—this… *insta*-family and—"

"And what?" He throws his hands up. "You don't want to have a family with me?"

"No, I do, but—"

"But what?"

How do I explain to him that in one brief conversation, Ginny Quick, of all people, peered into my soul, saw every one of my insecurities, and dangled them in front of my face until I could no longer see straight?

How do I tell him that I want him, but I'll be damned if I let myself *need* him?

He's completely stone-faced.

"You said once that you'd give me anything I need," I whisper and take his hand. "I'm so sorry, but this is what I need."

"Do what you need to do." He drops my hand and walks toward the door. Just before he's out of sight, he stops. He keeps his back to me when he says, "Colleen?"

I sniff. "Yeah?"

"I've been alone. Believe me, it's not all it's cracked up to be."

With a slam of the door, he's gone.

CHAPTER 22
BACON

WHEN YOUR DAD ABANDONS YOU AT EIGHT YEARS OLD AND YOUR mom all but relinquishes her parental rights when you're thirteen, you don't deal so well with the mother of your children moving out on you.

At least I'm not dealing so well.

But god knows I'm trying.

It's three and a half weeks until the restaurant's grand opening, so I have a million things to keep me busy, but still, all I can think about is her.

On day three of our separation, I open our text thread and read through all our messages from the past few months for what has to be the hundredth time, trying to understand where things went wrong.

Sam let me know she found a furnished one-bedroom apartment that had just opened up above Tiddy's.

You know things are bad when the pregnant mother of your children would rather live above a Tiddy bar than with you.

Double D, not double T. But still. It's bad.

Suddenly, three small dots pulse on her side of the text thread, signaling she's typing. My whole body goes on alert.

The dots appear and disappear several times before stopping entirely.

I guess she thought better about saying anything.

I put my phone down and rest my head in my hands on the main food prepping counter in my brand-new restaurant kitchen while my sous chef and a few other restaurant staff scurry around. The producers of *Yes, Chef!* made sure I have a wonderful staff. They took care of interviewing local folks from Fork Lick and surrounding towns so I could focus on the creative aspects of the proceedings. For anyone looking to launch a new restaurant, I highly recommend winning a reality TV cooking show first and getting this level of support. It's especially helpful when you're experiencing heartbreak and have a hard time getting your head on straight.

This afternoon, we have some early reviewers coming in to sample our fare, and hopefully, they will garner us some good press. I could use any kind of win right now to lift my spirits.

My phone buzzes against the metal prep table, startling me. I pick up immediately.

"Colleen?" I'm embarrassed by the eagerness in my tone.

"Sorry to disappoint, buddy. It's me."

"Trent! Hey, man. It's good to hear from you. How's the book tour going?"

"It's, uh—well, it's on a pause for now."

"On a pause? What the hell are you talking about? Your new book just came out this week."

"That it did." He sighs.

There's a heaviness on Trent's side of the phone.

"What am I missing, dude? You okay?"

"Yeah? I guess? Things are just kind of—"

"Spit it out, buddy," I joke.

"My dad died on Tuesday."

I don't have words right away. That's the last thing I

thought he was going to say. Trent's dad has always been this force of nature. And a beacon for me of what a real dad can be. When he and Trent's mom welcomed me into their home as a young teen, it's no exaggeration to say they saved my life. They gave me a home when I didn't have one. They gave me a family when my own had let me down so spectacularly. I owe much of who I am—and the father I plan to become—to that man.

"I'm sorry to drop the news like this. It was unexpected. I know he meant a lot to you."

"He did," I say softly. "He *does*." Shifting into past tense feels disrespectful somehow. "I'm shocked. And I'm so sorry, man. Is there anything I can do? How are you dealing?"

"Dealing okay, I think? I don't know. I'm back in Doylestown helping my mom with the bookstore until she's up for it again." Frustration creeps into his tone. "I've been telling them for years that they should sell it, but did they listen to me?"

"I'm glad you're there helping her out. She must be devastated," I say. "Their love story was one for the ages, right? Isn't that what your dad always said?"

"Yeah." Trent sniffs. "He did." He clears his throat. "Tell me something good. How's your lady and those babies she's incubating?"

Well Trent, on the exact day I planned to propose to her, she left me.

I'm not usually one to obfuscate the truth, but in this case, I feel it's warranted.

"We're great!" I say. "And the babies are doing great too. Doctors expect them to arrive a bit early. Apparently, twins almost always do."

"Oh, man, that's terrific. Congrats, buddy, I'm so happy for you."

"Thank you."

"You know, I owe you an apology," Trent says.

"For what?"

"For the way I tried to steer you away from her all those months ago, telling you to move on, forget her, blah, blah, blah. It turns out that was more about me and my own shitty history with relationships. You didn't need my negativity getting in your way. Clearly, you knew what you were doing all along. I'm glad you followed your gut and got the happy ending you deserve."

The happy ending isn't quite a done deal yet, not by a long shot, but I leave that part unsaid.

"Well, if you're going to blame yourself for that, it's only fair you give yourself credit for your woolen bra detective work that led me back to her in the first place."

"You're right," Trent jokes. "I do deserve credit for that!"

"You certainly do."

We laugh until Trent quickly gets serious again. "Listen, I know it's really short notice and you have a million things going on, but – "

"When are the services?" I ask.

"Tomorrow morning. Ten o'clock."

"I'll be there."

"Bacon. No one expects you to drop everything and—"

"Trent? Your dad gave me a home when I didn't have one. He treated me like a son when my real father couldn't be bothered. I'll be there."

———

Mourners pour out of the service for Trent's dad, their arms wrapped around each other, dabbing at their eyes with tissues. *Mourners* likely isn't the right word, though. Of course there is a sadness—a somberness—in the air, but what I just witnessed inside that funeral home was a celebration.

We celebrated the life of a kind and decent man. One by one, people came up to the podium and shared stories about the impact Trent's dad has had on their lives. By all accounts, he was a phenomenal husband, father, and friend who soaked up every moment possible with the people he loved. I count myself incredibly lucky that I was one of those people.

I couldn't take my eyes off Trent and his sister during those speeches as they nodded their heads and squeezed each other's hands. What an absolute gift it must be to hear such wonderful things said about your father and to know without a doubt that they're true.

That's not something I'll experience in my lifetime, but if I play my cards right, hopefully many years from now *my* children will.

I spot a bench outside the funeral home and take a seat. As soon as I sit, my phone vibrates in my pocket with a text.

COLLEEN

Is it too soon to say I miss you?

I respond immediately and without thinking.

No, but it doesn't change the fact that you left.

Maybe I'm being harsh. Maybe I should open my heart and say what I *really* want to say, which is, "I love you and I miss you so much it's killing me." Maybe I should tell her that I'm at a funeral for a man I adored, and it's bringing up a million questions for me like "Why couldn't my own father stick around?" and "Why do the people who love me always leave me?"

But I don't say any of those things. I just pocket my phone and close my eyes, hoping the spring sun shining down on me can provide some semblance of comfort.

Footsteps approach. Trent is coming down the steps with his mother and sister, the last ones to leave the service. I rise to greet them.

"Thank you again for being here, sweetheart," his mother says when they reach me. "Richard loved you very much and so do I."

"I love you too, Joanne." I give her another hug. "And Richie Rich. He was a wonderful man."

"He sure was. And he loved when you called him that." She dabs at her nose with a handkerchief. "We'll see you at the luncheon? Or do you have to head back to Fart Lick?"

I try to stifle my laugh, so it comes out as a snort. "It's, uh —It's *Fork* Lick, ma'am, not Fart Lick."

"Oh thank goodness!" She chuckles. "I was trying to be supportive of your new town's name, but I was struggling with it. *Fork* Lick is much better. May the patrons at your new comfort food restaurant happily lick their forks for years to come."

"Thank you, my friend." I place a hand on her shoulder. "I'd love you all to come up for a meal on the house when you're up for it."

"We certainly will, sweetheart. See you at the luncheon."

"I'll see you." I nod.

Trent's sister gives me a wink and ushers her mother toward their waiting car. After they're out of sight, Trent hangs back with an odd look on his face.

"You wanna ride with me?" I gesture to my car in the parking lot.

"Hell no," Trent jokes. "You're a terrible driver."

"A guy backs into a fire hydrant *one* time…" I joke back, but something about Trent is still off. "What's going on?" I ask. "You okay?"

"Yeah," he says. "All things considered, I'm okay. I just—I have something to say to you," he stammers. "And I hope you take it the way it's intended."

"Dude, you sound nervous." I chuckle. "When have you ever been nervous to say something to me?"

"Have you responded to any of those messages you were getting from your dad?" he blurts.

"No." The usual pit in my stomach that makes itself known whenever my father is mentioned rears its ugly head. "Why?"

"Maybe you should."

I sigh. "Trent. I know you're hurting with your dad passing, but your dad and the man who sired me—"

"Were *nothing* alike," he finishes the sentiment so I don't have to. "I'd never suggest that they were. If you were handed a shitty deal on the father front, then I won the fucking lottery. I know that. But I have been thinking—" I can tell he's trying to choose his words carefully, a rarity for Trent. "My sister mentioned something interesting the other day. She said that the instant she became a parent, she was flooded with all these unresolved feelings about her childhood. She said those feelings really messed with her head. And that's coming from someone who had an inarguably happy childhood. I'm just wondering if, for *you*, things could be even more intense."

"Trent," I protest.

"I'd just hate to see you work so hard to build this beautiful life with your wife and kids and then realize you have all this unresolved junk in your brain that messes with your ability to be a good, present dad."

"My wife, huh?" I huff sadly.

"Yeah," he says. "You plan on marrying this girl, don't you?"

I scrub my forehead with my hands. "Yeah. I have the ring and everything. But she's—" How do I explain this? "I think she's having cold feet about our relationship."

"Huh." Trent thinks a moment. "Well, you can't really blame her, can you?"

"How do you mean?"

"Things have moved really fast with you two. New relationship, new home, new restaurant, new babies—*plural*! That would be a lot for anyone. Maybe she just needs some time for her brain to catch up with her heart."

"Yeah, maybe," I say softly.

"But I'm not talking about Colleen right now. I'm talking about *you*. It might be wise to sort out some of your feelings about your dad before you become a dad yourself." He pauses. "Think about it, okay?"

"I have to say, this whole conversation is decidedly un-Trent-like."

Trent slaps a hand on my shoulder. "Believe me, Porky. I know. I guess losing someone puts some things into perspective." He continues, "And look, I'm not saying you need to forgive him—or that he even *deserves* that—but maybe it's worth hearing him out. To be open to the conversation. Not for him. For you."

I stare off into the distance and nod, taking in all that he's said.

"Alright." He pats my shoulder twice and releases me. "That's all the sensitivity and emotional maturity I can handle for one day. "See you at lunch, brother."

I sit back down on the bench and sigh as I watch Trent head to his car.

Brother.

That man *is* my brother. In every way that matters.

He gave me a family when I needed one. And today he might just have helped me repair the one I'm trying to build.

I wave to Trent as he drives away.

Then, for the first time in over a decade, I pull out my phone and call my father.

CHAPTER 23
COLLEEN

LAUGHTER, MUSIC, AND THE SOUND OF CLINKING GLASSES WAFTS through the floor as I try – and fail – to write something new.

I'm thirty-five-and-a-half weeks pregnant. I've been living alone in a crappy furnished rental apartment above a dive bar for nearly a month in my quest to be an "independent woman."

And you know what?

It sucks.

Bacon and I text every few days, but we mostly talk about my doctor's appointments and how the babies are progressing. Other than that, he's giving me the space I requested.

I hate every second of it.

The doorbell buzzer squeals, startling me like it does every time it rings. I run through the list of who it could be. My brothers visit regularly to tell me how stubborn I'm being. Lia, Molly, and Diane make appearances under the guise of "impromptu girls' nights," then inevitably encourage me to rethink this experiment of mine.

It could be any one of them at the door right now, but the most likely scenario is that a drunken Tiddy's patron is poking the buzzer for shits and giggles. It wouldn't be the first time. Or even the hundredth.

I walk to the front window and peel back the curtain to peer at the ground below. The last person I expected to see waits patiently at the entrance to my tenant stairwell.

I press the responding buzzer immediately, fling open the door to my apartment, and shout down the stairs. "Gran? What on earth are you doing here at nine o'clock at night?"

"Can't a girl enjoy a drink at the tittie bar then visit her granddaughter for some tea?" she says as she ascends the staircase with her usual grace and agility.

My brothers and I have long since stopped correcting Gran when she says titties instead of Tiddy's. It's not worth it at this point.

When she reaches my landing, I usher her inside and give her a hug. "You were having a drink at Tiddy's?" I say in disbelief. She breezes past me as I shut the door. "Whoa! Don't you look pretty? New dress?" I step closer to her. "And is that makeup I see?"

"Don't sound so shocked, Colleen. You know, I *can* look presentable sometimes." She does a little spin.

"You look presentable all the time. You're a beautiful woman, Gran. Today, your look is just a bit... elevated."

"Well, you kids always seem to enjoy those tittie trivia nights, so I decided to try one out." She hesitates. "And... I thought perhaps it might be a good place to meet some suitors."

"Oh. *Suitors.*" I take a moment for that to settle in. "Wow."

"Maybe that's silly, but—"

"No, ma'am." I shake my head. "That's not silly at all. I think it's wonderful that you're feeling ready to get back out there."

"You don't think your grandfather would mind?" Gran stares down at her shoes. Suddenly, she seems so much younger than her seventy-one years.

"No," I say definitively. "I don't. I think he would be happy seeing you living your life to the fullest."

A small smile spreads across Gran's face when she looks me in the eyes again. "How about that tea?"

"Sure, have a seat." I turn on the kettle and grab my small stash of tea bags from a cabinet.

I don't tell her this, but I'm so happy she's here. I miss seeing her whenever I want to. When I was living with her at Bedd Fellows, she was the first person I saw in the morning and the last person I saw at night. And when I moved into the church loft with Bacon, all I had to do was look out the window, and I could see the light on in her bedroom just down the hill. I don't think I realized how much comfort that gave me until it went away. Until *I* went away.

"I have chamomile, peppermint, and red raspberry leaf. Which would you like?"

"I thought the raspberry leaf wasn't safe for pregnancy?" Gran says.

"It is now." I rub my truly massive belly. "I'm almost thirty-six weeks. Softening the cervix is now the name of the game."

"Raspberry leaf it is then, sugar!" She shoots me with a rapid-fire of finger guns.

"You're calling me 'sugar'? And busting out finger guns?" I laugh. "What's gotten into you, grandmother?" I place tea bags into the only two mugs I own and set them on the table. I stay standing while I wait for the water to boil.

Gran leans back in her chair. "Oh, just a little something I picked up from The Geezers. Big John, Little John, Small Paul, and Tall Paul all send their best to you, by the way."

"That's nice," I say.

Maybe I should head down to trivia again some night and spend time with human beings other than the ones I'm currently gestating.

I started early maternity leave from Fork Lick Elementary last week. My doctor suggested it, saying that the last few weeks of carrying twins can get super uncomfortable, so I'd be wise to prioritize rest. I took his advice, though my actual plan was to prioritize *writing* and see if I could lay the groundwork to actually make a career out of this thing. The proof copy of my first book is due any day now—and I'm so proud of that—but I haven't written a single quality word since I left Bacon.

Turns out, being around him, being in love with him, being *happy*… that was the creative inspiration I needed.

Gran drums her fingers on the wooden table and gazes around the space. I can feel her disapproval when her eyes land on the scuffed laminate countertops, the faded creaky floorboards, and the conspicuous water stain spreading on the ceiling. "So. Are you done yet with the self-imposed torture game you've been putting yourself through?" she says.

"I don't know what you mean." I turn to the squealing kettle.

"You know exactly what I mean." Gran stares me down like she used to when I was a kid and left the freezer door open. "This nonsense about needing to be on your own. Moving out of the lovely home you've created with Bacon."

"Gran, were you or were you not the person who told me just a few months ago that I should focus on writing?" I pour hot water into both of our mugs, return the kettle to the stove, and sit down beside her.

"That was me, yes. But at no point did I say you had to move out on the man you love in order to do it. I swear, young people today are so extreme! It's all or nothing with you kids!"

"For the last time, Gran, I needed to prove that I could be on my own. That I could rely *only* on myself." I've tried explaining this to her many times, but she just doesn't get it. "Over and over again in my life, I've let people save me. My parents died? You and Granddad stepped in to take care of me. Girls were bullying me at school? The Bedd brothers came to my rescue. I got pregnant from a one-night stand? A gorgeous man swooped in with a beautiful new home for me to live in and all but begged to support me financially. Not only that, but he came up with a whole plan for how he can contribute to my family's failing farm."

Gran interjects, "Well now, I wouldn't say our farm is *failing*. We've hit some bumps in the road, but—"

"I'm tired of taking the easy way out!" I shout.

You could hear a pin drop after my outburst.

Rule #1 in our house growing up: you do not raise your voice to Gran.

"Colleen Bedd," Gran says softly after a few moments of silence.

"Gran, I'm sorry I yelled, I'm just—"

"You're just going to listen to me right now. That's what you're going to do," she says fiercely. "I heard you say your piece. Now it's your turn to hear me say mine."

"Yes, ma'am," I say.

"I want you to hear me very closely, young lady. You, Colleen Bedd, have never taken the easy way out. Never."

"But—"

"Never," she repeats. "You were ten years old when you lost your parents. That is a terrible tragedy to have to face. And you faced it with more grace than people five times your age could have managed. You certainly handled it better than I did."

"But, Gran, you lost your *son*. I can't imagine what that must have been like." I place my hands on my belly. "I haven't even met these two yet, and just the thought of losing them makes me—" My voice breaks, and I swipe at my eyes. I can't bear to even finish that thought.

Gran's eyes go glassy. "It was an incredibly difficult time, and I mourn your father to this day. But in case I've never told you this outright, I need you to know: it was my honor to step up and become your primary parent. You and your brothers—and now these two great-grandbabies—are the joy of my life. You are the blessings I was given after a great storm."

"That's…" I grab a tissue from the table and blow my nose. "That's beautiful, Gran."

"It's the truth." She shifts gears from sadness to her usual no-nonsense attitude. "Now, I'd like you to reflect on what you said a moment ago. Every example you gave of taking the easy way out was actually just someone loving you. Your grandfather and I raised you because we love you. Your brothers defended and protected you because they love you. And that very sexy Bacon boy of yours? He wants to build a life with you because he loves you." She reaches across the table and covers my hand with hers. "Let people love you."

The light tap of a truck horn sounds from outside.

Gran gets to her feet. "That's your eldest brother. He and Lia brought me tonight and are driving me home." She walks to the window with her mug and peels back the curtain. She waves to them. "Can't say I'm too fond of being beeped at, but I suppose I'll let this one slide."

"You?" I chuckle. "You're going to let something slide?"

She shrugs. "None of us love each other perfectly. What matters is that we try."

"You're getting wise in your old age, Gran."

She points a finger at me. "Don't kid yourself, missy. I've been wise at *every* age."

I laugh and blow my nose again. "You're right. You have."

She takes a sip from her mug and winces. "Though I was dead wrong about this beverage. Red Raspberry leaf tea tastes like dirt." She pours her tea out in the sink. "Can I scrub this mug before I go?"

"No, no, I'll get it. Ethan's waiting for you." I unlock and open the door.

Gran joins me in the doorway, her purse slung over her arm.

"One last thing?" she says with a smile.

I sigh. "Sure, Gran. What is it?"

She cups my cheeks with her soft, warm hands. "You're allowed to need people, sweetheart. No one gets a medal for getting through life alone."

She's right.

She's always right.

I nod. "Good night, Gran. I love you."

"I love you too, dear. Very much."

I wait until she's down the stairwell before I shut and lock the door again. I peel back the curtain and wave to Ethan as he guides Gran into his truck.

No one gets a medal for getting through life alone.

I take a deep breath and swipe at my eyes one more time.

Then I pick up my phone and send a text.

> Can we talk? Like really talk?

CHAPTER 24
BACON

It's the night before the restaurant opening.

The tables are set. The food is prepped. The menus are stacked and waiting at the host station.

Everything is ready.

Bella Keegan exits from the back office and joins me in the main dining area, where I'm sitting on a barstool surveying the space. "How are you feeling, chef? Nervous?"

Bella is an event specialist the *Yes, Chef!* team brought onboard for our opening. She's originally from Bayshore, Ohio, and she's a master at creating events big and small, whether it's a restaurant launch in a small town like Fork Lick, NY, or a Super Bowl performance in the biggest stadiums in the country. She's staying in the main house at Bedd Fellows with Ethel while we wrap up this launch.

"A bit, yeah," I say. "But the nerves are nowhere near the intensity level I had on the set of *Yes, Chef!*" Or on the stage at Constitution High School in Philadelphia, for that matter.

"Remember, no one expects you to 'perform,'" Bella says. "Your team has the tough stuff covered. All you have to do tomorrow is show up, smile pretty, and cook."

"It's almost as if you could pull this off without me," I joke. "Should I just stay home?"

"Don't even think about it." She points a finger at me. "Though last time I checked, your home is right up those stairs. So in the event that you do pull a no-show, I don't have to go very far to find you."

"I'll be here, Bella. I promise." I let out a breath. "I just hope *she* will be too."

Bella places a friendly hand on my back. "Listen. I've only just started getting to know these future in-laws of yours. But staying with Ethel these past few weeks has taught me a bit about the Bedd family. From what I've observed, they're stubborn and they fight hard, but they love harder." She gives me a friendly pat. "I'm betting on you and Colleen."

"Thanks, Bella. For everything. You've been a lifesaver throughout this process."

She shrugs like it's no big deal. "Eh. It's what I do." She grabs her laptop and a few stacks of papers from the bar. "See you tomorrow, boss?"

"See you tomorrow."

She lets herself out and heads down the hill to Bedd Fellows Farm.

Just as I'm about to shut off the lights and head upstairs for the night, a text chimes on my phone.

COLLEEN

Can we talk? Like really talk?

Absolutely. Give me five minutes. I'll be right there.

I grab my keys and hightail it to the exit, my heart pounding with excitement. When I swing the door open, a man with salt-and-pepper hair and weathered skin stands in front of me, his fist raised to knock.

"Dad?" I say in disbelief.

The man's face splits into a grin. "Hello, Harry."

"You sure that's all you want to drink?" I ask Harold Senior as we sit across from one another for the first time in years. "We have a stocked bar."

"No, no." He waves a hand and sips from the glass I gave him. "Water is fine." He scans the interior of the restaurant. "Quite a place you got here, kid. Am I allowed to say I'm proud of you?"

I pause before responding. "You're *allowed* to say whatever you want, I suppose."

He nods. "Well then, I'm proud of you."

We sit silently for a minute, neither knowing what to say next.

It's the oddest thing, looking at the man partially responsible for my existence and feeling like a stranger to him.

"You know, I called you a few weeks ago," I say. "Emailed you too."

"Did you?" He seems pleased. "Appreciate that. I've been on the road for the past month or so. You know me. I like to keep moving."

"You don't check your cell?" I ask. "I called the number you gave me in your letters. I left voicemails."

"You know me, I don't believe in cell phones."

"Why not?"

"That's how they track ya." He laughs, but as the child he left behind, I don't find it very funny. He continues, "The number I gave you was my ex's landline. I was with her at the time, but I don't live there anymore." He shrugs. "What can I say? Relationships are rough. Anyway, I saw the articles circulating about your success. Thought I owed it to ya to swing by and say 'good on ya.'"

"You thought you *owed* it to me?"

"Well, you know me, I—"

I have to interrupt. "You keep saying that. 'You know me.' But that's the thing. I *don't* know you. Never have."

"I guess you're right. I, uh—I'm sorry about that?" He scrubs a hand through his wiry hair. "Turns out I'm not much of a family man, I guess."

I sigh. "Yeah, I guess not."

Seeing him now, he looks way older than his sixty years. I almost feel bad for him. Here's a guy who's spent his whole life running, never slowing down enough to realize the good that's all around him. Always looking for something better. And he doesn't appear to be any closer to finding it.

We have the same lips and deep brown eyes, but that's where the similarities end.

"Look," I say. "I called because I have something I need to say to you."

"So say it, kid."

"Alright. Uh—" I clear my throat. "If you'd shown up a year ago—or even three months ago—I'd have had some choice words for you. I would have told you that you screwed up. That you didn't do right by Mom. That you missed out on having a relationship with me. But I'm not going to do that now. You know why?"

"Why?" His eyes soften, and for the first time since he walked in, his bravado slips away, and he seems to really be listening.

"Because despite how my life started, I'm doing great now. I'm done letting your actions dictate how I feel about myself and how I show up in the world." I sigh. "God, I spent so much time telling myself I'm alone, that until recently, I never stopped to truly recognize how many people *do* care about me. Do you remember the Cartwrights?"

"I think so." He squints as he thinks. "Richard and Joanne?"

"That's right." I nod. "Richard and Joanne. And their kids

Trent and Autumn too. They've been there for me since I was fifteen years old. They took me in when I didn't have anywhere else to go."

"I'll have to pay them a visit sometime and thank them," he says.

"Richard just passed," I tell him. "But he was a good man. A 'family man' to use your words."

A flash of hurt—or maybe just acceptance—flashes across my father's face. It's not my intention to hurt him. But after all these years, these things need to be said.

I continue, "Richard's son, Trent, was the one who encouraged me to reach out to you. To get some of these things off my chest. He didn't want me going into fatherhood with the past still dragging me down."

"You're going to be a father?" he says in surprise.

"I am." I smile. "Next month. Two babies, actually. A boy and a girl."

"Wow. Congratulations, kid." His eyes actually well up. "Do, uh—Do a better job than I did, will ya?"

"I will." I nod resolutely.

"Well…" Harold Senior says after a moment of silence. He gets to his feet with some effort. "I've taken up enough of your time for one night."

I stand and follow him to the door. I open it for him.

"Thank you for coming to see me tonight, Dad. I imagine it took some courage on your part."

"Maybe one of these days we'll see each other again," he says hopefully.

"Yeah, maybe." I extend a hand to him. "Be safe out there."

He shakes my hand, gives me a wink, and heads toward a beat-up truck parked a little way down the road.

As I watch him drive away, I don't feel angry. I don't feel resentful or lost or any of the other feelings that used to arise when I think of my father. I feel... peace. I think of Colleen and the family we're creating together, and I'm more determined than ever to make things right.

CHAPTER 25
COLLEEN

I'M SITTING IN GRAN'S KITCHEN WITH MY LAPTOP, DRESSED AS nicely as I can manage in my uber-pregnant state.

Bacon never showed up at my apartment last night.

He said he'd be over in five minutes, and he never showed.

When I woke up this morning, all I had was this simple text:

> **BACON**
>
> Something came up tonight. My head is spinning. Will talk tomorrow.

I came to Gran's an hour ago to walk over to Bacon's restaurant opening together, but now I'm wondering if he even wants me there. I'm not going to let that deter me from my plan, though. His head may be spinning, but mine is crystal clear now. We belong together. And today, I'm going to show him why.

I just need a very important package to arrive first.

Perhaps it's telling that I forwarded my mail to Gran's house this month instead of directly to my rental apartment. I couldn't bring myself to make this living arrangement official in any way.

I check the shipping status on my book order for what has to be the hundredth time this hour.

The message still reads: *Shipped. Due to arrive today by 4 p.m.*

"It's officially four o'clock, fuckers!" I yell. "Where the hell is it?"

Gran walks into the kitchen at that exact inopportune moment. "Colleen Murphy Bedd. For the last time, language! My great-grandchildren can hear you!"

"You're right, Gran, I'm sorry." I rub my large-and-in-charge belly. "Sorry, kiddos. Mommy will do better."

A car rumbling up the drive has us both looking out the window.

"That's Molly and Alex here to escort us to the opening," Gran says. "Get your shoes on, missy. It's time to get your man."

"I have every intention of getting my man," I say, "but I need this book to be delivered first so I can bring it with me. It factors into my whole plan for getting him back."

Gran gives me a doubtful look.

"I promise I'll be there. As soon as it arrives, I'll walk over." I pause. "Gran, I wrote it for him. I don't want to just *tell* him how much I love him. I want to *show* him."

"Kids today." She shakes her head, but I see her smile as she shuts the door behind her.

After I watch Alex walk across the field with Molly and Gran, I'm left alone in the kitchen, willing the delivery truck to appear.

A dull pang aches in my belly again. I've been getting these on and off since late last night. They're not painful exactly. More like a tightening and relaxing every few minutes. I called Climax OB-GYN this morning to make sure this is normal. When I described the sensation to them, they said at thirty-four weeks pregnant, they were most likely

Braxton Hicks contractions and nothing to worry about. They told me to call again if they intensified.

Another pang hits me, a little sharper this time.

I close my eyes and breathe through it.

Just then, the front doorbell rings.

By the time get to the door, I see the delivery truck pulling out of our drive and onto the street.

"It's here!" I shout to no one. I look down past our front steps, and right next to our bright yellow flowerpot is a flat rectangular cardboard box holding my first-ever published children's book inside.

I try to ignore the pangs in my belly as I sit down on the middle step and tear into the package.

Collie and Porky's Great Adventure is emblazoned on the cover above an illustration of a little girl Border collie dog and a little boy potbellied pig. Underneath the image are the glorious words "by Colleen Murphy Bedd."

Happy tears stream down my cheeks as I flip through the book. Every word I wrote gleams up at me from the glossy pages, filling me with pride unlike I've ever felt before.

Just then, Baabara saunters up beside me. And because I want to share my happiness with *someone*—and for some reason, my biggest life moments always seem to involve this sheep—I say, "Hey, girl! Come look."

Big mistake.

Baabara looks at the book, alright. And then she promptly snatches it in her slobbery muzzle and hauls sheep ass around the side of the house.

"No!" I scream. "Bad sheep! Bad!"

I leap to my feet and experience the strongest, sharpest pang in my belly yet.

Either pregnant women shouldn't be leaping or I'm in labor.

I need to call Bacon.

But I also need to catch that damn sheep.

"Baabara!" I walk as quickly as I can in the direction I saw her last. "Baabara, get back here this minute! Baabara!"

When I turn the corner, Bacon holds my rambunctious sheep by the scruff of her neck. "Hi," he says. "Seemed like you could use a little help."

I run up to him, kiss him, and hug him for dear life.

And that's when my water breaks.

All over his designer shoes.

CHAPTER 26
BACON

"DID YOU JUST PEE ON ME?" I ASK.

She looks down.

"I don't, uh—I don't know. Maybe? I'm sorry, Bacon. For everything. For leaving you—both times—for making you work so hard to love me, and now..." I look down at his shoes. "...for peeing on you. I love you, *and* I need you, Bacon. I'm not afraid to say it anymore. I, Colleen Murphy Bedd need you Harold "Bay-CAHN" Hotman with every fiber of my being. I need to see your beautiful face every day. I need your warmth and your kindness and your touch of weird. Mostly I need you to know that I love you and I want to spend the rest of my life with you. Gosh, did I really just pee on you?"

"Let me make something very clear to you, Colleen. You have never been hard to love, and nothing would make me happier than for you to pee on me for the rest of our lives."

"Ha! God, I love you." She grabs her belly and winces while she speaks. "Yup, these are getting super strong now."

"What are getting super strong now?" I try to hide my panic, but I am wholly unsuccessful. I also let go of the sheep. "Colleen, are you in labor!?"

"Affirmative," she says through the pain. "Also, I'm real-izing that was my water breaking on your shoes just now."

"But we're only thirty-five-and-a-half weeks!" I say.

"They told us twins usually come early."

"Sure, but not this early!"

"It's okay," she soothes. "Everything is going to be okay."

It occurs to me then that I have to get my shit together immediately. Colleen is in full labor, and *she's* comforting *me*.

"Alright, I'll run up the hill to the restaurant and pull the car around. We'll have you at the hospital before you know it."

"The hospital is over a half hour away in Climax. I know I've never done this whole giving birth thing before, but I'm pretty sure we don't have time."

"What makes you say that?"

She reaches under her skirt. "Because I can feel one of the babies' heads."

Holy shit. Holy shit. Holy shit.

"Baaa!" the sheep bleats from her fancy sheep palace, almost like she's beckoning us. "Baaaa!"

"That's a great idea, Baabara, thank you," Colleen says, still gripping her belly. "Bacon, can you help me walk over to Baabara's enclosure?"

"You're going to give birth in Barbara's pen? Also, you speak sheep?" I loop an arm behind Colleen's back and guide her in that direction.

"Baaa!" the sheep bleats louder than the last time.

"She's yelling at you," Colleen says. "You pronounced her name wrong. You've really gotta hit the *Baaa* part, or you risk pissing her off."

"Sure, sure. This is a perfectly reasonable discussion to be having while our children are being born. Let me rephrase for the sheep. You're going to give birth in Baaaaaaaaaaaaaabara's pen?"

"If it's good enough for Baabara, it's good enough for me," she says. "Quick, put that blanket down over the hay."

"Is it sanitary, though?"

"Baabara is the most pampered sheep on the planet. Her linens are laundered every day."

I spread the thick plaid blanket on the ground.

Colleen gets down on all fours.

"Okay," I say. "What now? What do you need?"

She takes a deep breath in and an even deeper breath out. "I need to push."

CHAPTER 27
COLLEEN

"And Collie and Porky lived on the farm together happily ever after," I say as Bacon turns the last page and closes the book. "What do you think?"

Bacon's eyes are filled with happy tears. "You wrote a book about us." Bacon shakes his head in wonder. "That is the coolest thing anyone's ever done for me. You know, besides giving me a son and a daughter on the very same day."

"Do you get it, though?" I ask shyly, not used to sharing my work. "Did the message come through?"

"A girl Border collie named Collie who's spent her life herding her brothers and a potbellied pig named Porky who lost his parents finding love and friendship on a farm?" He laughs. "It's pretty clear. Some would even say it's 'on the nose.'" He taps me gently on the nose with his index finger, then kisses my forehead. "I absolutely love it." He stares down at our babies. "And I know these two will love it too."

As soon as we entered Baabara's pen, Bacon called 911. As far as birth plans go, I can't say that I recommend our approach, but ultimately, it was wonderful. We had a beautiful natural birth on the farmlands I love, then we were whisked away by paramedics to make sure the babies and I got the medical attention we needed.

Now, we're side by side, propped up in my surprisingly cozy hospital bed, and each holding a healthy, sleeping newborn.

The doctors and nurses were pleasantly surprised by how big and robust the babies were for only being thirty-five and a half weeks.

"I'm sorry you missed your opening," I say.

"I'm not." He gives me another kiss, this time on my lips. "We have a great staff. They knew what to do."

"How did you end up where I needed you when I needed you?"

"As soon as your family showed up at the restaurant without you, I decided I'd had enough of missing you. I stormed down to Bedd Fellows, prepared to tell you, that's it, woman! Me and my pork sword have suffered enough!"

A nurse quickly knocks and enters just in time to hear Bacon's pork sword comment. His face immediately goes red. "My apologies, ma'am. That was inappropriate."

She waves a hand. "Don't even mention it. The things we see and hear in this place would blow your mind." She approaches the bed and peeks at the babies. "We still doing okay here?"

"Great, yes. It's normal for them to be sleeping this much, right?" I ask.

"Oh, yes. Enjoy these early, sleepy days, Mom. Because one day, they wake up and are ready for a nonstop party. That's when the real fun begins."

"Can't wait," Bacon says, and I know he means it.

He is so excited to be a father.

"So. Mom and Dad," the nurse says. "There is quite a crew out in the waiting room who wants to see you. Ordinarily, we only allow four visitors at a time, but I think we can make a small exception for the winner of *Yes, Chef!* and his lovely family. Just don't tell my boss."

"That's very sweet of you," Bacon says. "But you don't have to bend the rules for—"

"What he meant to say was, 'Thanks for watching the show. We can't wait to see you at our new restaurant in Fork Lick. Tell the hostess you know the chef, and she'll get you your first round of drinks for free.'" I lower my voice to a whisper. "And thank you for bending the rules for us. Can you give us a few minutes and then let them in?"

"I sure can." The nurse winks. "Thank you for the generous offer. My wife and I can't wait to visit. Be back soon with your crew."

My crew. I like the way she says that. They are my crew, and I can't wait for them to meet our newest two. But I need to ask Bacon something first.

"Don't you want to get your family in here right away?" Bacon says. "Why are you making them wait?"

"Last night—when you didn't show up—you said your head was spinning." I pause. "I just want to make sure we're truly okay."

"Cookie?" He looks deep into my eyes. "We're golden. That wasn't because of you. I, uh—I saw my father last night."

"What? Are you serious? How did that happen? How did it go? How do you feel?"

He chuckles. "Slow down, sister. Trent encouraged me to reach out. He said a lot of people have unresolved feelings rise up about their childhoods when they become parents. I didn't want any of my… stuff to affect you and the kids. He'd been sending me messages on and off for years, so I finally responded. Long story short, he didn't get my voicemails, but he saw an article about the restaurant and just showed up."

"And how was it?"

"It was… fine. Finally talking to him and seeing him face-to-face… released all this tension I didn't realize I'd been holding." He strokes our son's tiny head. "I don't have to forgive him or let him be a grandfather to our bacon bits. But who knows? We left the door open. So maybe one day—if we find our footing—he can be their weird uncle or something."

"Like they don't already have enough of those," I laugh.

"True," he says. "Well, time will tell, I guess."

"But you feel better?" I ask. "That's all that matters."

He sighs. "I do. I do feel better."

"Knock, knock," Gran's singsong voice wafts into the room. "Have room for a few visitors?"

"We sure do," I singsong back.

Ethan, Lia, Alex, Molly, Sam, and Diane all file in quietly behind Gran and gather around us.

"Come in, everybody. Come meet Cassandra Jane and Daniel James."

Ethan speaks first. "Cassandra as in—?"

"Sandra. Yeah," I say. "We wanted to honor Mom while still giving little Cassie her own name. And her middle name Jane is for Bacon's mom."

Gran smiles. "Beautiful, sweetheart. Just beautiful."

"And Daniel?" Sam gets choked up with emotion, a rarity for him.

"That one's for you, buddy. We wanted to honor the man who taught me how to twin, the babies' awesome Uncle Sam-Dan."

Without a word, Sam rushes to my side and rests his head on my shoulder.

I pat him on the cheek. "Love you, brudder."

"Love you too, Collie," he whispers back. "Thank you."

"And his middle name, James…" I continue.

"…is for Dad," Alex says.

"Thank you for honoring my Jimmy," Gran says.

"You bet, Gran," I say. "Thank you for being you."

EPILOGUE

COLLEEN

"A BLINDFOLD? ARE YOU SERIOUS RIGHT NOW?" I SAY AS I timidly shuffle-step toward what I think is the restaurant's back entrance with a handkerchief tied across my eyes. Bacon leads me by the hand, wearing one-week-old Cassie and Danny strapped to his chest in our fancy new double carrier. "You do realize I've seen what the restaurant looks like before," I joke.

"Yes, but you haven't seen the improvements the staff and I made over the past week while the babies were still in the hospital."

Since the babies were born at thirty-five-and-a-half weeks —a tad earlier than twins are expected—the doctors thought it best that they stay under observation until it was deemed safe to discharge them. I've basically been by their sides nonstop, even showering and sleeping at the hospital.

Today is the monumental day we bring our bacon bits home.

When we exited the car a moment ago, Bacon asked if I wouldn't mind taking a quick detour into the restaurant before heading upstairs to the nursery. I'm exhausted, and my nipples are threatening to break off with the epic amount of breastfeeding I've been doing, but he looked too excited by whatever he has planned that I couldn't bear to tell him no.

The restaurant doesn't open for lunch for another hour, so it's fairly quiet when Bacon leads me into the space. All I can hear are the faint sounds of the kitchen staff in the back and the occasional clink of silverware while the front-of-house staff sets the tables.

"Alright. First thing's first." Bacon stops us in what feels like the center of the space and puts something in my hands.

"What is this?" I ask. "The menu?"

"Take off the blindfold," he encourages.

"It *is* the menu." I scan it and don't see anything out of the ordinary. "I don't get it. Did you update some of the dishes?"

"No." He laughs. "Look at the top, will ya?"

"*Cassie and Danny's Place*," I read out loud, then it hits me. "Oh, my goodness. You changed the name of the restaurant? Are you allowed to do that?"

"I'm the owner. I can do whatever I want."

"Sure, but won't it cause confusion? You've been open for a week with the original name!"

"Turns out *Bacon Bits* was confusing for people. They assumed it was one of those chichi places that only served one thing. Plus, I thought this was a more effective way to celebrate the twins. I would have suggested it right away, but someone told me announcing babies' names before they're born is bad luck."

"Bacon, this is incredible." I kiss him, then whisper to our sleeping babies cradled on their father's chest. "Did you hear that Cassie and Danny? You have your own restaurant." I give them a quick kiss on their tiny bald heads and look back up at Bacon. "So it's official, then?"

He nods. "As you saw, new menus are already printed. A press release is going out this morning, and our new outside signage will arrive this week."

"Amazing," I say, completely in awe.

"Think you can handle one more surprise? Well, possibly two, depending on how you look at it. Actually, I guess it's technically three. You know what? No. I think it's four."

"What are you talking about?" I laugh.

"Remember that small back room we weren't entirely sure what to do with? We thought it could be used for private parties, but it's not quite big enough?"

"Bacon, yes. I've had baby brain these past few weeks, but I haven't forgotten whole conversations about your business!" I playfully scold.

"*Our* business," he corrects. He's always doing that, making sure I know that whatever is his is mine as well. "We're a team."

"Yes, we are," I agree.

"Well, I found a use for it. Should I blindfold you again?" He hesitates. "Nah. Just come back here with me."

He takes me into the back room, and what I see honest-to-god takes my breath away.

The entire room is lined with floor-to-ceiling bookshelves, just like the ones he had back in his New York City apartment.

"Bacon..." I breathe. "Is it a library?"

He smiles. "Sort of, yeah. I thought it would be nice for people to have a place to relax and read with their kids after their meal. This wasn't all me, though. Bella was instrumental in setting this all up."

"I'll be sure to thank her. But how did you get all these books?" I marvel.

"We have Gran to thank for that one. She posted a TikTok asking all her followers to donate books to us. Boy, that lady is getting a lot of traction on that platform. Anyway, the donations just keep pouring in. The adult section is here..." He gestures to the left corner. We've got mysteries, thrillers, romance, biographies, fiction, non-fiction... you name it. And the kids' section is over here." He points at the far wall filled with brightly covered children's books. There are even plush chairs and tiny reading lamps creating the perfect child-size reading nooks.

"This is so—I can't believe you—" I don't finish my thought because what I see next literally makes me weak in the knees.

Bacon steadies me and guides me to a simple wooden table where at least a hundred copies of my children's book are placed in neat stacks. Beside them, a small silver cup filled with black permanent markers stands at the ready.

"You ordered a gazillion copies of my book?"

He shrugs. "Had to. Today is your first book signing."

"My first what?" I squeal.

"Look out the window," he says.

A long line of Fork Lickers has assembled outside the restaurant, and Bella is handing out copies of my book.

"What in the world is happening right now?" I want to add some happy expletives to that question, but much to Gran's delight, I have managed to clean up my language just a tad in honor of my new motherhood.

"You don't mind signing a few copies, do you?" he asks as he guides me to the soft armchair positioned behind the table. "They paid online. All proceeds are going to The Bedd Fellows Family Fund, which is basically just a separate bank account I started so we can keep doing our part to pay off the farm debt."

"You are something else, Hotman."

He winks. "Back atcha, Bedd. What do you say? Can I let them in?"

"Please," I say excitedly. "Yes!"

I take a seat and pick up a pen, then instantly drop it and leap to my feet when the first person enters the room. He's trying to be incognito with a baseball cap and dark sunglasses, but I'd know my kid brother anywhere.

"Jackie Boy! Oh my—What are you doing here?" I squeeze him in the tightest hug.

"I heard my big sister wrote a book and had some babies," Jackson says. "There's no way I was going to miss all that."

"This had better be the last surprise, Bacon," I say, my arms still wrapped tightly around my little brother. "I don't think I can take any more."

"I can confirm that Jackson is, in fact, the last surprise. I saved the best for last."

"Thanks, man," Jackson says. "I knew I liked you."

I guide Jackson closer to Bacon and our two sleeping bundles of joy. "Cassie? Danny?" I whisper. "This is my baby brother, Jackson. Think you can handle one more uncle?"

———

Want more Colleen and Bacon? My newsletter subscribers get an exclusive bonus scene of their happily ever after. Go to erinmallon.com/home#connect and subscribe!

FARM 2 FORKING SERIES

Bedd Fellows Farm is in trouble. Grandad bequeathed the five Bedd siblings a heap of debt, along with a troublesome sheep, and they're all too stubborn to accept the help they need to dig their way out of the compost pile.

Join authors Lainey Davis, Liz Alden, Karen Grey, Erin Mallon, and Ember Leigh as they share un-baa-lievable tales of love, laughter, and sexy shenanigans, all set in the bucolic fictional town of Fork Lick, New York.

Meddling grandmas, nosy neighbors, and boinking abound in these steamy romantic comedies.

Since You've Bean Gone by Lainey Davis
Butter You Up by Liz Alden
For Fork's Sake by Karen Grey
Bringing Home the Bacon by Erin Mallon
A Fork in the Road by Ember Leigh

MORE FROM THE AUTHORS

Catch up with the Bedds' neighbors in the Planted and Plowed series by Lainey Davis. Asher Thorne is the hero of Sappy Go Lucky.

Take your romcoms with a side of wanderlust. Kit gets his own story in the upcoming Anywhere But Here series by Liz Alden. In the meantime, check out Aged Like Fine Wine, where four best friends explore Europe and love after forty!

Stayed tuned for a new small town romcom series coming soon from Karen Grey, set down the road from Fork Lick and kicking off with single dad Ben's story! In the meantime, check out her nostalgic romance at karengrey.com.

As a girl with four brothers, Colleen Bedd knows what it's like to be "one of the guys." For more strong heroines who aren't afraid to go head-to-head with their fellas, dive into The Natural History Series by Erin Mallon.

Jackson's leading lady hails from Bayshore, a small, lakeside Ohio town that sets the stage for Ember's other rom-coms.

Visit Bayshore now to meet the Daly brothers, and to get ready for the next series launching soon.

ACKNOWLEDGMENTS

My goodness this has been a fun ride!

Thank you first and foremost to the wonderful Karen Grey, who brought me into this merry band of authors. There's no one else I'd rather create a set of literary twins with than you! Sometimes the best things in life are surprises (Just ask Colleen and Bacon about their surprise "bacon bits!") and this experience was no exception. I wasn't planning on co-creating a family and a farm and all sorts of sheep shenanigans this year, but when someone invites you to a great party, you RSVP yes! I'm so glad I did.

Thank you to Lainey Davis for her unwavering positivity, friendship, and encouragement.

Thank you to Liz Alden for her smart feedback, generous spirit, and formatting prowess.

Thank you to Ember Leigh for being an absolute baller, birthing a book and a baby in the same week!

I'd also like to thank the great Jenny Sims of Editing4Indies. Knowing your expert eyes are on my books gives me such comfort! Jodi Martin and Julia Heudorf, your beta brilliance means the world to me, thank you.

As always, Keith and our Three Js have my heart.

Last but certainly not least, thank you, readers, for embracing my work and getting onboard with a hero named Bacon. You let me be weird and that is the greatest gift.

9 781736 925881